John H. Aughey

# The Iron Furnace

SALZWASSER
VERLAG

**John H. Aughey**

# The Iron Furnace

Reprint of the original, first published in 1863.

1st Edition 2022 | ISBN: 978-3-37500-219-0

Verlag (Publisher): Salzwasser Verlag GmbH, Zeilweg 44, 60439 Frankfurt, Deutschland
Vertretungsberechtigt (Authorized to represent): E. Roepke, Zeilweg 44, 60439 Frankfurt, Deutschland
Druck (Print): Books on Demand GmbH, In de Tarpen 42, 22848 Norderstedt, Deutschland

# THE IRON FURNACE:

OR,

# SLAVERY AND SECESSION.

BY

REV. JOHN H. AUGHEY,

A REFUGEE FROM MISSISSIPPI.

Cursed be the man that obeyeth not the words of this covenant, which I commanded your fathers in the day that I brought them forth out of the land of Egypt, from the *Iron Furnace*.—Jer. xi. 3, 4. See also, 1 Kings viii. 51.

PHILADELPHIA:

1863.

Engraved by Samuel Sartain, Phila.

John H. Aughey.

# PREFACE.

A celebrated author thus writes: "Posterity is under no obligations to a man who is not a parent, who has never planted a tree, built a house, nor written a book." Having fulfilled all these requisites to insure the remembrance of posterity, it remains to be seen whether the author's name shall escape oblivion.

It may be that a few years will obliterate the name affixed to this Preface from the memory of man. This thought is the cause of no concern. I shall have accomplished my purpose if I can in some degree be humbly instrumental in serving my country and my generation, by promoting the well-being of my fellow-men, and advancing the declarative glory of Almighty God.

This work was written while suffering intensely from maladies induced by the rigours of the Iron Furnace of Secession, whose seven-fold heat is reserved for the loyal citizens of the South. Let this fact be a palliation for whatever imperfections the reader may meet with in its perusal.

There are many loyal men in the southern States, who to avoid martyrdom, conceal their opinions. They are to be pitied—not severely censured. All those southern ministers and professors of religion who were eminent for piety, opposed secession till the States passed the secession ordinance. They then advocated reconstruction as long as it comported with their safety. They then, in the face of danger and death, became quiescent—not acquiescent, by any means—and they now "bide their time," in prayerful trust that God will, in his own good time, subvert rebellion, and overthrow anarchy, by a restoration of the supremacy of constitutional law. By these, and their name is legion, my book will be warmly approved. My fellow-prisoners in the dungeon at Tupelo, who may have survived its horrors, and my fellow-sufferers in the Union cause throughout the South, will read in my narrative a transcript of their own sufferings. The loyal citizens of the whole country will be interested in learning the views of one who has been conversant with the rise and progress of secession, from its incipiency to its culmination in rebellion and treason. It will also doubtless be of general interest to learn something of the workings of the "peculiar institution," and the various phases which it assumes in different sections of the slave States.

Compelled to leave Dixie in haste, I had no time to collect materials for my work. I was therefore under the necessity of writing without those aids which would have secured greater accuracy. I have done the best that I could under the circumstances; and any errors that may have crept into my statements of facts, or reports of addresses, will be cheerfully rectified as soon as ascertained.

That I might not compromise the safety of my Union friends who rendered me assistance, and who are still within the rebel lines, I was compelled to omit their names, and for the same reason to describe rather indefinitely some localities, especially the portions of Ittawamba, Chickasaw, Pontotoc, Tippah, and Tishomingo counties, through which I travelled while escaping to the Federal lines. This I hope to be able to correct in future editions.

Narratives require a liberal use of the first personal pronoun, which I would have gladly avoided, had it been possible without tedious circumlocution, as its frequent repetition has the appearance of egotism.

I return sincere thanks to my fellow-prisoners who imperilled their own lives to save mine, and also to those Mississippi Unionists who so generously aided a panting fugitive on his way from chains and death to life and liberty. My thanks are also due to Rev. William P. Breed, for assistance in preparing my work for the press.

I am also under obligations to Rev. Francis J. Collier, of Philadelphia; to Rev. A. D. Smith, D. D., and Rev. J. R. W. Sloane, of New York, and to Rev. F. B. Wheeler, of Poughkeepsie, New York.

May the Triune God bless our country, and preserve its integrity!

JOHN HILL AUGHEY.

FEBRUARY 1, 1863.

# CONTENTS.

## CHAPTER I.

### SECESSION.



## CHAPTER II.

### VIGILANCE COMMITTEE AND COURT-MARTIAL.



## CHAPTER III.

### ARREST, ESCAPE, AND RECAPTURE.

## CHAPTER IV.

### LIFE IN A DUNGEON.



## CHAPTER V.

### EXECUTION OF UNION PRISONERS.

## CHAPTER VI.

### SUCCESSFUL ESCAPE.



## CHAPTER VII.

### SOUTHERN CLASSES—CRUELTY TO SLAVES.

## CHAPTER VIII.

### NOTORIOUS REBELS.—UNION OFFICERS.



## CHAPTER IX.

### CONDITION OF THE SOUTH.



## CHAPTER X.

### BATTLES OF LEESBURG, BELMONT, AND SHILOH.

# THE IRON FURNACE;

OR

# SLAVERY AND SECESSION.

## CHAPTER I.

### SECESSION.

**Speech of Colonel Drane.—Submission Denounced.—Northern Aggression.—No more Slave States.—Northern *isms*.—Yankees' Servants.—Yankee inferiority.—Breckinridge, or immediate, complete, and eternal Separation.—A Day of Rejoicing.—Abraham Lincoln President elect.—A Union Speech.—A Southerner's Reasons for opposing Secession.—Address by a Radical Secessionist.—Cursing and Bitterness.—A Prayer.—Sermon against Secession.—List of Grievances.—Causes which led to Secession.**

At the breaking out of the present rebellion, I was engaged in the work of an Evangelist in the counties of Choctaw and Attala in Central Mississippi. My congregations were large, and my duties onerous. Being constantly employed in ministerial labours, I had no time to intermeddle with politics, leaving all such questions to statesmen, giving the complex issues of the day only sufficient attention to enable me to vote intelligently. Thus was I engaged when the great political campaign of 1860 commenced—a campaign conducted with greater virulence and asperity than any I have ever witnessed. During my casual detention at a store, Colonel Drane arrived, according to appointment, to address the people of Choctaw. He was a member of one of my congregations, and as he had been long a leading statesman in Mississippi, having for many years presided over the State Senate, I expected to hear a speech of marked ability, unfolding the true issues before the people, with all the dignity, suavity, and earnestness of a gentleman and patriot; but I found his whole speech to be a tirade of abuse against the North, commingled with the bold avowal of treasonable sentiments. The Colonel thus addressed the people:

MY FELLOW-CITIZENS—I appear before you to urge anew resistance against the encroachments and aggressions of the Yankees. If the

Black Republicans carry their ticket, and Old Abe is elected, our right to carry our slaves into the territories will be denied us; and who dare say that he would be a base, craven submissionist, when our God-given and constitutional right to carry slavery into the common domain is wickedly taken from the South. The Yankees cheated us out of Kansas by their infernal Emigrant Aid Societies. They cheated us out of California, which our blood-treasure purchased, for the South sent ten men to one that was sent by the North to the Mexican war, and thus we have no foothold on the Pacific coast; and even now we pay five dollars for the support of the general Government where the North pays one. We help to pay bounties to the Yankee fishermen in New England; indeed *we* are always paying, paying, paying, and yet the North is always crying, Give, give, give. The South has made the North rich, and what thanks do we receive? Our rights are trampled on, our slaves are spirited by thousands over their underground railroad to Canada, our citizens are insulted while travelling in the

North, and their servants are tampered with, and by false representations, and often by mob violence, forced from them. Douglas, knowing the power of the Emigrant Aid Societies, proposes squatter sovereignty, with the positive certainty that the scum of Europe and the mudsills of Yankeedom can be shipped in in numbers sufficient to control the destiny of the embryo State. Since the admission of Texas in 1845, there has not been a single foot of slave territory secured to the South, while the North has added to their list the extensive States of California, Minnesota, and Oregon, and Kansas is as good as theirs; while, if Lincoln is elected, the Wilmot proviso will be extended over all the common territories, debarring the South for ever from her right to share the public domain.

The hypocrites of the North tell us that slaveholding is sinful. Well, suppose it is. Upon us and our children let the guilt of this sin rest; we are willing to bear it, and it is none of their business. We are a more moral people than they are. Who originated Mormonism, Millerism, Spirit-rappings, Abolitionism, Free-loveism, and all the other abominable *isms* which curse the world? The reply is, the North. Their puritanical fanaticism and hypocrisy is patent to all. Talk to us of the sin of slavery, when the only difference between us is that our slaves are black and theirs white. They treat their white slaves, the Irish and Dutch, in a cruel manner, giving them during health just enough to purchase coarse clothing, and when they become sick, they are turned off to starve, as they do by hundreds every year. A female servant in the North must have a testimonial of good character before she will be employed; those with whom she is labouring will not give her this so long as they desire her services; she therefore cannot leave them, whatever may be her treatment, so that she is as much compelled to remain with her employer as the slave with his master.

Their servants hate them; our's love us. My niggers would fight for me and my family. They have been treated well, and they know it.

And I don't treat my slaves any better than my neighbours. If ever there comes a war between the North and the South, let us do as Abraham did—arm our trained servants, and go forth with them to the battle. They hate the Yankees as intensely as we do, and nothing could please our slaves better than to fight them. Ah, the perfidious Yankees! I cordially hate a Yankee. We have all suffered much at their hands; they will not keep faith with us. Have they complied with the provisions of the Fugitive Slave Law? The thousands and tens of thousands of slaves aided in their escape to Canada, is a sufficient answer. We *have* lost millions, and *are* losing millions every year, by the operations of the underground railroad. How deep the perfidy of a people, thus to violate every article of compromise we have made with them! The Yankees are an inferior race, descended from the old Puritan stock, who enacted the Blue Laws. They are desirous of compelling us to submit to laws more iniquitous than ever were the Blue Laws. I have travelled in the North, and have seen the depth of their depravity. Now, my fellow-citizens, what shall we do to resist Northern aggression? Why simply this: if Lincoln or Douglas are elected, (as to the Bell-Everett ticket, it stands no sort of chance,) let us secede. This remedy will be effectual. I am in favour of no more compromises. Let us have Breckinridge, or immediate, complete, and eternal separation.

The speaker then retired amid the cheers of his audience.

Soon after this there came a day of rejoicing to many in Mississippi. The booming of cannon, the joyous greeting, the soul-stirring music, indicated that no ordinary intelligence had been received. The lightnings had brought the tidings that Abraham Lincoln was President elect of the United States, and the South was wild with excitement. Those who had been long desirous of a pretext for secession, now boldly advocated their sentiments, and joyfully hailed the election of Mr. Lincoln as affording that pretext. The conservative men were filled with gloom. They regarded the election of Mr. Lincoln, by the majority of the people of the United States, in a constitutional way, as affording no cause for secession. Secession they regarded as fraught with all the evils of Pandora's box, and that war, famine, pestilence, and moral and physical desolation would follow in its train. A call was made by Governor Pettus for a convention to assemble early in January, at Jackson, to determine what course Mississippi should pursue, whether her policy should be submission or secession.

Candidates, Union and Secession, were nominated for the convention in every county. The speeches of two, whom I heard, will serve as a specimen of the arguments used *pro* and *con*. Captain Love, of Choctaw, thus addressed the people.

MY FELLOW-CITIZENS—I appear before you to advocate the Union—the Union of the States under whose favoring auspices we have long prospered. No nation so great, so prosperous, so happy, or so much respected by earth's thousand kingdoms, as the Great Republic, by which name the United States is known from the rivers to the ends of the earth. Our flag, the star-spangled banner, is respected on every sea, and affords protection to the citizens of every State, whether amid the pyramids of Egypt, the jungles of Asia, or the mighty cities of Europe. Our Republican Constitution, framed by the wisdom of our Revolutionary fathers, is as free from imperfection as any document drawn up by uninspired men. God presided over the councils of that convention which framed our glorious Constitution. They asked wisdom from on high, and their prayers were answered. Free speech, a free press, and freedom to worship God as our conscience dictates, under our own vine and fig-tree, none daring to molest or make us afraid, are some of the blessings which our Constitution guarantees; and these prerogatives, which we enjoy, are features which bless and distinguish us from the other nations of the earth. Freedom of speech is unknown amongst them; among them a censorship of the press and a national church are established.

Our country, by its physical features, seems fitted for but one nation. What ceaseless trouble would be caused by having the source of our rivers in one country and the mouth in another. There are no natural boundaries to divide us into separate nations. We are all descended from the same common parentage, we all speak the same language, and we have really no conflicting interests, the statements of our opponents to the contrary notwithstanding. Our opponents advocate separate State secession. Would not Mississippi cut a sorry figure among the nations of the earth? With no harbour, she would be dependent on a foreign nation for an outlet. Custom-house duties would be ruinous, and the republic of Mississippi would find herself compelled to return to the Union. Mississippi, you remember, repudiated a large foreign debt some years ago; if she became an independent nation, her creditors would influence their government to demand payment, which could not be refused by the weak, defenceless, navyless, armyless, moneyless, repudiating republic of Mississippi.

To pay this debt, with the accumulated interest, would ruin the new republic, and bankruptcy would stare us in the face.

It is true, Abraham Lincoln is elected President of the United States. My plan is to wait till Mr. Lincoln does something unconstitutional. Then let the South unanimously seek redress in a constitutional manner. The conservatives of the North will join us. If no redress is made, let us present our ultimatum. If this, too, is rejected, I for one will not advocate submission; and by the coöperation of all the slave States, we will, in the event of the perpetration of wrong, and a refusal to redress our grievances, be much abler to secure our rights, or to defend them at the cannon's mouth and the point of the bayonet. The Supreme Court favours the South. In the Dred Scott case, the Supreme Court decided that the negro was not a citizen, and that the slave was a chattel, as we regard him. The majority of Congress on joint ballot is still with the South. Although we have something to fear from the views of the President elect and the Chicago platform, let us wait till some overt act, trespassing upon our rights, is committed, and all redress denied; then, and not till then, will I advocate extreme measures.

Let our opponents remember that secession and civil war are synonymous. Who ever heard of a government breaking to pieces without an arduous struggle for its preservation? I admit the right of revolution, when a people's rights cannot otherwise be maintained, but deny the right of secession. We are told that it is a reserved right. The constitution declares that all rights not specified in it are reserved to the people of the respective States; but who ever heard of the right of total destruction of the government being a reserved right in any constitution? The fallacy is evident at a glance. Nine millions of people can afford to wait for some overt act. Let us not follow the precipitate course which the ultra politicians indicate. Let W. L. Yancey urge his treasonable policy of firing the Southern heart and precipitating a revolution; but let us follow no such wicked advice. Let us follow the things which make for peace.

We are often told that the North will not return fugitive slaves. Will secession remedy this grievance? Will secession give us any more slave territory? No free government ever makes a treaty for the rendition of fugitive slaves—thus recognising the rights of the citizens of a foreign nation to a species of property which it denies to its own citizens. Even little Mexico will not do it. Mexico and Canada return no fugitives. In the event of secession, the United States would return no fugitives, and our peculiar institution would, along our vast border, become very insecure; we would hold our slaves by a very slight tenure. Instead of extending the great Southern institution, it would be contracting daily. Our slaves would be held to service at their own option, throughout the whole border, and our gulf States would soon become border States; and the great insecurity of this species of property would work, before twenty years, the extinction of slavery, and, in consequence, the ruin of the South. Are we prepared for such a result? Are we prepared for civil war? Are we prepared for all the evils attendant upon a fratricidal contest — for bloodshed, famine, and political and moral desolation? I reply, we are not; therefore let us look before we leap, and avoiding the heresy of secession—

> "Rather bear the ills we have,
> Than fly to others that we know not of."

A secession speaker was introduced, and thus addressed the people:

LADIES AND GENTLEMEN—FELLOW-CITIZENS—I am a secessionist out and out; voted for Jeff Davis for Governor in 1850, when the same issue was before the people; and I have always felt a grudge against the *free state* of Tishomingo for giving H. S. Foote, the Union candidate, a majority so great as to elect him, and thus retain the State in this accursed Union ten years longer. Who would be a craven-hearted, cowardly, villanous submissionist? Lincoln, the abominable, white-livered abolitionist, is President elect of the United States; shall he be permitted to take his seat on Southern soil? No, never! I will volunteer as one of thirty thousand, to butcher the villain if ever he sets foot on slave territory. Secession or submission! What patriot would hesitate for a moment which to choose? No true son of Mississippi would brook the idea of submission to the rule of the baboon Abe Lincoln—a fifth-rate lawyer, a broken-down hack of a politician, a fanatic, an abolilitionist. I, for one, would prefer an hour of virtuous liberty to a whole eternity of bondage under northern, Yankee, wooden-nutmeg rule. The halter is the only argument that should be used against the submissiouists, and I predict that it will soon, very soon, be in force.

We have glorious news from Tallahatchie. Seven tory-submissionists were hanged there in one day, and the so-called Union candidates, having the wholesome dread of hemp before their eyes, are not canvassing the county; therefore the heretical dogma of submission, under any circumstances, disgraces not their county. Compromise! let us have no such word in our vocabulary. Compromise with the Yankees, after the election of Lincoln, is treason against the South; and still its syren voice is listened to by the demagogue submissionists. We should never have made any compromise, for in every case we surrendered rights for the sake of peace. No concession of the scared Yankees will now prevent secession. They now understand that the South is in earnest, and in their alarm they are proposing to yield us much; but the die is cast, the Rubicon is crossed, and our determination shall ever be, No union with the flat-headed, nigger-stealing, fanatical Yankees.

We are now threatened with internecine war. The Yankees are an inferior race; they are cowardly in the extreme. They are descended from the Puritan stock, who never bore rule in any nation. We, the descendants of the Cavaliers, are the Patricians, they the Plebeians. The Cavaliers have always been the rulers, the Puritans the ruled. The dastardly

Yankees will never fight us; but if they, in their presumption and audacity, venture to attack us, let the war come—I repeat it—let it come! The conflagration of their burning cities, the desolation of their country, and the slaughter of their inhabitants, will strike the nations of the earth dumb with astonishment, and serve as a warning to future ages, that the slaveholding Cavaliers of the sunny South are terrible in their vengeance. I am in favour of immediate, independent, and eternal separation from the vile Union which has so long oppressed us. After separation, I am in favour of non-intercourse with the United States so long as time endures. We will raise the tariff, to the point of prohibition, on all Yankee manufactures, including wooden-nutmegs, wooden clocks, quack nostrums, &c. We will drive back to their own inhospitable clime every Yankee who dares to pollute our shores with his cloven feet. Go he must, and if necessary, with the bloodhounds on his track. The scum of Europe and the mudsills of Yankeedom shall never be permitted to advance a step south of 36° 30′. South of that latitude is ours—westward to the Pacific. With my heart of hearts I hate a Yankee, and I will make my children swear eternal hatred to the whole Yankee race. A mongrel breed—Irish, Dutch, Puritans, Jews, free niggers, &c.—they scarce deserve the notice of the descendants of the Huguenots, the old Castilians, and the Cavaliers. Cursed be the day when the South consented to this iniquitous league—the Federal Union—which has long dimmed her nascent glory.

In battle, one southron is equivalent to ten northern hirelings; but I regard it a waste of time to speak of Yankees—they deserve not our attention. It matters not to us what they think of secession, and we would not trespass upon your time and patience, were it not for the tame, tory submissionists with which our country is cursed. A fearful retribution is in waiting for the whole crew, if the war which they predict, should come. Were they then to advocate the same views, I would not give a fourpence for their lives. We would hang them quicker than old Heath would hang a tory. Our Revolutionary fathers set us a good example in their dealings with the tories. They sent them to the shades infernal from the branches of the nearest tree. The North has sent teachers and preachers amongst us, who have insidiously infused the leaven of Abolitionism into the minds of their students and parishioners; and this submissionist policy is a lower development of the doctrine of Wendell Philips, Gerritt Smith, Horace Greely, and others of that ilk. We have a genial clime, a soil of uncommon fertility. We have free institutions, freedom for the white man, bondage for the black man, as nature and nature's God designed. We have fair women and brave men. The lines have truly fallen to us in pleasant places. We have indeed a goodly heritage. The only evil we can complain of is our bondage to the Yankees through the Federal Union. Let us burst these shackles from our limbs, and we will be free indeed.

Let all who desire complete and eternal emancipation from Yankee thraldom, come to the polls on the —— day of December, prepared not to vote the cowardly submissionist ticket, but to vote the secession ticket; and their children, and their children's children, will owe them a debt of gratitude which they can never repay. The day of our separation and vindication of States' rights, will be the happiest day of our lives. Yankee domination will have ceased for ever, and the haughty southron will spurn them from all association, both governmental and social. So mote it be!

This address was received with great eclat.

On the next Sabbath after this meeting, I preached in the Poplar Creek Presbyterian church, in Choctaw county, from Romans xiii. 1: "Let every soul be subject unto the higher powers. For there is no power but of God: the powers that be, are ordained of God."

Previous to the sermon a prayer was offered, of which the following is the conclusion:

ALMIGHTY GOD—We would present our country, the United States of America, before thee. When our political horizon is overcast with clouds and darkness, when the strong-hearted are becoming fearful for the permanence of our free institutions, and the prosperity, yea, the very existence of our great Republic, we pray thee, O God, when flesh and heart fail, when no human arm is able to save us from the fearful vortex of disunion and revolution, that thou wouldst interpose and save us. We confess our national sins, for we have, as a nation, sinned grievously. We have been highly favoured, we have been greatly prospered, and have taken our place amongst the leading powers of the earth. A gospel-enlightened nation, our sins are therefore more heinous in thy sight. They are sins of deep ingratitude and presumption. We confess that drunkenness has abounded amongst all classes of our citizens. Rulers and ruled have been alike guilty; and because of its wide-spreading prevalence, and because our legislators have enacted no sufficient laws for its suppression, it is a national sin. Profanity abounds amongst us; Sabbath-breaking is rife; and we have elevated unworthy men to high positions of honour and trust. We are not, as a people, free from the crime of tyranny and oppression. For these great and aggravated offences, we pray thee to give us repentance and godly sorrow, and then, O God, avert the threatened and imminent judgments which impend over our beloved country. Teach our Senators wisdom. Grant them that wisdom which is able to make them wise unto salvation; and grant also that wisdom which is profitable to direct, so that they may steer the ship of State safely through the troubled waters which seem ready to engulf it on every side. Lord, hear us, and answer in mercy, for the sake of Jesus Christ our Lord. Amen and Amen!

The following is a synopsis of my sermon:

Israel had been greatly favoured as a nation. No weapon formed against them prospered, so long as they loved and served the Lord their God. They were blessed in their basket and their store. They were set on high above all the nations of the earth. * * * *

When all Israel assembled, ostensibly to make Rehoboam king, they were ripe for rebellion. Jeroboam and other wicked men had fomented and cherished the sparks of treason, till, on this occasion, it broke out into the flame of open rebellion. The severity of Solomon's rule was the pretext, but it was only a pretext, for during his reign the nation prospered, grew rich and powerful. Jeroboam wished a disruption of the kingdom, that he might bear rule; and although God permitted it as a punishment for Israel's idolatry, yet he frowned upon the wicked men who were instrumental in bringing this great evil upon his chosen people.

The loyal division took the name of Judah, though composed of the two tribes, Judah and Benjamin. The revolted ten tribes took the name of their leading tribe, Ephraim. Ephraim continued to wax weaker and weaker. Filled with envy against Judah, they often warred against that loyal kingdom, until they themselves were greatly reduced. At last, after various vicissitudes, the ten tribes were carried away, and scattered and lost. We often hear of the lost ten tribes. What became of them is a mystery. Their secession ended in their being blotted out of existence, or lost amidst the heathen. God alone knows what did become of them. They resisted the powers that be—the ordinance of God—and received to themselves damnation and annihilation.

As God dealt with Israel, so will he deal with us. If we are exalted by righteousness, we will prosper; if we, as the ten tribes, resist the ordinance of God, we will perish. At this time, many are advocating the course of the ten tribes. Secession is a word of frequent occurrence. It is openly advocated by many. Nullification and rebellion, secession and treason, are convertible terms, and no good citizen will mention them with approval. Secession is resisting the powers that be, and therefore it is a violation of God's command. Where do we obtain the right of secession? Clearly not from the word of God, which enjoins obedience to all that are in authority, to whom we must be subject, not only for wrath, but also for conscience' sake. The following scriptural argument for secession is often used, 1 Tim. vi. 1—5. In these verses Paul was addressing believing servants, and commanding them to absent themselves from the teaching of those who taught not the doctrine which is according to godliness. In a former epistle he had commanded Christians not to keep company with the incestuous person who had his father's wife. He directed that they should not keep company with any man who was called a brother, if he were a fornicator, or covetous, or an idolator, or a railer, or a drunkard, or an extortioner; with such a one no not to eat; but he expressly declares that he does not allude to those who belong to the above classes that have made no profession of religion. He does not judge them that are without, for them that are without, God judgeth. He afterwards exhorts that the church confirm their love toward the incestuous person as he had repented of his wickedness. This direction of the Apostle to believers to withdraw from a brother who walked disorderly, till he had manifested proper repentance; and his exhortation to believing servants to absent themselves from the teachings of errorists, cannot logically be construed as a scriptural argument in favour of secession. Were the President of the United States an unbeliever, a profane swearer, a Sabbath-breaker, or a drunkard, this fact would not, *per se*, give us the right to secede or rebel against the government.

There is no provision made in the Constitution of the United States for secession. The wisest statesmen, who made politics their study, regarded secession as a political heresy, dangerous in its tendencies, and destructive of all government in its practical application. Mississippi, purchased from France with United States gold, fostered by the nurturing care, and made prosperous by the wise administration of the general government, proposes to secede. Her political status would then be anomalous. Would her territory revert to France? Does she propose to refund the purchase-money? Would she become a territory under the jurisdiction of the United States Congress?

Henry Clay, the great statesman, Daniel Webster, the expounder of the Constitution, General Jackson, George Washington, and a mighty host, whose names would fill a volume, regarded secession as treason. One of our smallest States, which swarmed with tories in the Revolution, whose descendants still live, invented the doctrine of nullification, the first treasonable step, which soon culminated in the advocacy of secession. Why should we secede, and thus destroy the best, the freest, and most prosperous government on the face of the earth? the government which our patriot fathers fought and bled to secure. What has Mississippi lost by the Union? I have resided seven years in this State, and have an extensive personal acquaintance, and yet I know not a single individual who has lost a slave through northern influence. I have, it is true, known of some ten slaves who have run away, and have not been found. They may have been aided in their escape to Canada by northern and southern citizens, for there are many in the South who have given aid and comfort to the fugitive; but the probability is that they perished in the swamps, or were destroyed by the bloodhounds.

The complaint is made that the North regards slavery as a moral, social, and political evil, and that many of them denounce, in no measured terms, both slavery and slaveholders. To be thus denounced is regarded as a great grievance. Secession would not remedy this evil. In order to cure it effectually, we must seize and gag all who thus denounce our peculiar institution. We must also muzzle their press. As this is impracticable, it would be well to come to this conclusion:—If we are verily guilty of the evils charged upon us, let us set about rectifying those evils; if not, the denunciations of slanderers should not affect us so deeply. If our northern brethren are honest in their convictions of the sin of slavery, as no doubt many of them are, let us listen to their arguments without the dire hostility so frequently manifested. They take the position that slavery is opposed to the inalienable rights of the human race; that it originated in piracy and robbery; that manifold cruelties and barbarities are inflicted upon the defenceless slaves; that they are debarred from intellectual culture by State laws, which send to the penitentiary those who are guilty of instructing them; that they are put upon the block and sold; parent and child, husband and wife being separated, so that they never again see each other's face in the flesh; that the law of chastity cannot be observed, as there are no laws punishing rape on the person of a female slave; that when they escape from the threatened cat-o'-nine-tails, or overseer's whip, they are hunted down by bloodhounds, and bloodier men; that often they are half-starved and half-clad, and are furnished with mere hovels to live in; that they are often murdered by cruel overseers, who whip them to death, or overtask them, until disease is induced, which results in death; that masters practically ignore the marriage relation among slaves, inasmuch as they frequently separate husband and wife, by sale or removal; that they discourage the formation of that relation, preferring that the offspring of their female slaves should be illegitimate, from the mistaken notion that it would be more numerous. They charge, also, that slavery induces in the masters, pride, arrogance, tyranny, laziness, profligacy, and every form of vice.

The South takes the position, that if slavery is sinful, the North is not responsible for that sin; that it is a State institution, and that to interfere with slavery in the States in any way, even by censure, is a violation of the rights of the States. The language of our politicians is, Upon us and our children rest the evil! We are willing to take the responsibility, and to risk the penalty! You will find evil and misery enough in the North to excite your philanthropy, and employ your beneficence. You have purchased our cotton; you have used our sugar; you have eaten our rice; you have smoked and chewed our tobacco—all of which are the products of slave-labour. You have grown rich by traffic in these articles; you have monopolized the carrying trade, and borne our slave-produced products to your shores. Your northern ships, manned by northern men, brought from Africa the greater part of the slaves which came to our continent, and they are still smuggling them in. When, finding slavery unprofitable, the northern States passed laws for gradual emancipation, but few obtained their freedom, the majority of them being shipped South and sold, so that but few, comparatively, were manumitted. If the slave trade and slavery are great sins, the North is *particeps criminis*, and has been from the beginning.

These bitter accusations are hurled back and forth through the newspapers; and in Congress, crimination and recrimination occur every day of the session. Instead of endeavouring to calm the troubled waters, politicians are striving to render them turbid and boisterous. Sectional bitterness and animosity prevail to a fearful extent; but secession is not the proper remedy. To cure one evil by perpetrating a greater, renders a double cure necessary. In order to cure a disease, the cause should be known, that we may treat it intelligently, and apply a proper remedy. Having observed, during the last eleven years, that sectional strife and bitterness were increasing with fearful rapidity, I have endeavoured to stem the torrent, so far as it was possible for individual effort to do so. I deem it the imperative duty of all patriots, of all Christians, to throw oil upon the troubled waters, and thus save the ship of State from wreck among the vertiginous billows.

Most of our politicians are demagogues. They care not for the people, so that they accomplish their own selfish and ambitious schemes. Give them power, give them money, and they are satisfied. Deprive them of these, and they are ready to sacrifice the best interests of the nation to secure them. They excite sectional animosity and party strife, and are willing to kindle the flames of civil war to accomplish their unhallowed purposes. They tell us that there is a conflict of interest between the free and slave States, and endeavour to precipitate a revolution, that they may be leaders, and obtain positions of trust and profit in the new government which they hope to establish. The people would be dupes indeed to abet these wicked demagogues in their nefarious designs. Let us not break God's command, by resisting the ordinance of God—the powers that be. I am not discussing the right of revolution, which I deem a sacred right. When human rights are invaded, when life is endangered, when liberty is taken away, when we are not left free to pursue our own happiness in our own chosen way—so far as we do not trespass upon the rights of others—we have a right, and it becomes our imperative duty to resist to the bitter end, the tyranny which would deprive us and our children of our inalienable rights. Our lives are secure; we have freedom to worship God. Our liberty is sacred; we may pursue happiness to our hearts' content. We do not even charge upon the general Government that it has infringed these rights. Whose life has been endangered, or who has lost his liberty by the action of the Government? If that man lives, in all this fair domain of ours, he has the right to complain.

But neither you nor I have ever heard of or seen the individual who has thus suffered. We have therefore clearly no right of revolution.

Treason is no light offence. God, who rules the nations, and who has established governments, will punish severely those who attempt to overthrow them. Damnation is stated to be the punishment which those who resist the powers that be, will suffer. Who wishes to endure it? I hope none of my charge will incur this penalty by the perpetration of treason. You yourselves can bear me witness that I have not heretofore introduced political issues into the pulpit, but at this time I could not acquit my conscience were I not to warn you against the great sin some of you, I fear, are ready to commit.

Were I to discuss the policy of a high or low tariff, or descant upon the various merits attached to one or another form of banking, I should be justly obnoxious to censure. Politics and religion, however, are not always separate. When the political issue is made, shall we, or shall we not, grant license to sell intoxicating liquors as a beverage? the minister's duty is plain; he must urge his people to use their influence against granting any such license. The minister must enforce every moral and religious obligation, and point out the path of truth and duty, even though the principles he advocates are by statesmen introduced into the arena of political strife, and made issues by the great parties of the day. I see the sword coming, and would be derelict in duty not to give you faithful warning. I must reveal the whole counsel of God. I have a message from God unto you, which I must deliver, whether you will hear, or whether you will forbear. If the sword come, and you perish, I shall then be guiltless of your blood. As to the great question at issue, my honest conviction is (and I think I have the Spirit of God,) that you should with your whole heart, and soul, and mind, and strength, oppose secession. You should talk against it, you should write against it, you should vote against it, and, if need be, you should fight against it.

I have now declared what I believe to be your

high duty in this emergency. Do not destroy the government which has so long protected you, and which has never in a single instance oppressed you. Pull not down the fair fabric which our patriot fathers reared at vast expense of blood and treasure. Do not, like the blind Samson, pull down the pillars of our glorious edifice, and cause death, desolation, and ruin. Perish the hand that would thus destroy the source of all our political prosperity and happiness. Let the parricide who attempts it receive the just retribution which a loyal people demand, even his execution on a gallows high as Haman's. Let us also set about rectifying the causes which threaten the overthrow of our government. As we are proud, let us pray for the grace of humility. As a State, and as individuals, we too lightly regard its most solemn obligations; let us, therefore, pray for the grace of repentance and godly sorrow, and hereafter in this respect sin no more. As many transgressions have been committed by us, let the time past of our lives suffice us to have wrought the will of the flesh, and now let us break off our sins by righteousness, and our transgressions by turning unto the Lord, and he will avert his threatened judgments, and save us from dissolution, anarchy, and desolation.

If our souls are filled with hatred against the people of any section of our common country, let us ask from the Great Giver the grace of charity, which suffereth long and is kind, which envieth not, which vaunteth not itself, is not puffed up, does not behave itself unseemly, seeketh not her own, is not easily provoked, thinketh no evil; rejoiceth not in iniquity, but rejoiceth in the truth; beareth all things, believeth all things, hopeth all things, endureth all things, and which never faileth; then shall we be in a suitable frame for an amicable adjustment of every difficulty; oil will soon be thrown upon the troubled waters, and peace, harmony, and prosperity would ever attend us; and our children, and our children's children will rejoice in the possession of a beneficent and stable government, securing to them all the natural and inalienable rights of man.

## CHAPTER II.

### VIGILANCE COMMITTEE AND COURT-MARTIAL.

**The election of Delegates to determine the status of Mississippi—The Vigilance Committee—Description of its members—Charges—Phonography—No formal verdict—Danger of Assassination—Passports—Escape to Rienzi—Union sentiment—The Conscript Law—Summons to attend Court-Martial—Evacuation of Corinth—Destruction of Cotton—Suffering poor—Relieved by General Halleck.**

SOON after this sermon was preached, the election was held. Approaching the polls, I asked for a Union ticket, and was informed that none had been printed, and that it would be advisable to vote the secession ticket. I thought otherwise, and going to a desk, wrote out a Union ticket, and voted it amidst the frowns and suppressed murmurs of the judges and by-standers, and, as the result proved, I had the honour of depositing the only vote in favour of the Union which was polled in that precinct. I knew of many who were in favour of the Union, who were intimidated by threats, and by the odium attending it from voting at all. A majority of secession candidates were elected. The convention assembled, and on the 9th of January, 1861, Mississippi had the unenviable reputation of being the first to follow her twin sister, South Carolina, into the maelstrom of secession and treason. Being the only States in which the slaves were more numerous than the whites, it became them to lead the van in the slave-holders' rebellion. Before the 4th of March, Florida, Alabama, Georgia, Louisiana and Texas had followed in the wake, and were engulfed in the whirlpool of secession.

It was now dangerous to utter a word in favour of the Union. Many suspected of Union sentiments were lynched. An old gentleman in Winston county was arrested for an act committed twenty years before, which was construed as a proof of his abolition proclivities. The old gentleman had several daughters, and his mother-in-law had given him a negro girl. Observing that his daughters were becoming lazy, and were imposing all the labour upon the slave, he sent her back to the donor, with a statement of the cause for returning her. This was now the ground of his arrest, but escaping from their clutches, a precipitate flight alone saved his life.

Self-constituted vigilance committees sprang up all over the country, and a reign of terror began; all who had been Union men, and who had not given in their adhesion to the new order of things by some public proclamation, were supposed to be disaffected. The so-called Confederate States, the new power, organized for the avowed purpose of extending and perpetuating African slavery, was now in full blast. These *soi-disant* vigilance committees professed to carry out the will of Jeff. Davis. All who were considered disaffected were regarded as being tinctured with abolitionism. My opposition to the disruption of the Union being notorious, I was summoned to appear before one of these august tribunals to answer the charge of being an abolitionist. My wife was very much alarmed, knowing that were I found guilty of the charge, there was no hope for mercy. Flight was impossible, and I deemed it the safest plan to appear before the committee. I found it to consist of twelve persons, five of whom I knew, viz., Parson Locke, Armstrong, Cartledge, Simpson, and Wilbanks. Parson Locke, the chief speaker, or rather the inquisitor-general, was a Methodist minister, though he had fallen into disrepute among his brethren, and was engaged in a tedious strife with the church which he left in Holmes county. The parson was a real Nimrod. He boasted that in five months he had killed forty-eight raccoons, two hundred squirrels, and ten deer; he had followed the bloodhounds, and assisted in the capture of twelve runaway negroes. W. H. Simpson was a ruling elder in my church. Wilbanks was a clever sort of old gentleman, who had little to say in the matter. Armstrong was a monocular Hard-shell-Baptist. Cartledge was an illiterate, conceited individual. The rest were a motley crew, not one of whom, I feel confident, knew a letter in the alphabet. The committee assembled in an old carriage-shop. Parson Locke acted as chairman, and conducted the trial, as follows.

"Parson Aughey, you have been reported to us as holding abolition sentiments, and as being disloyal to the Confederate States."

"Who reported me, and where are your witnesses?"

"Any one has a right to report, and it is optional whether he confronts the accused or not. The proceedings of vigilance committees are somewhat informal."

"Proceed, then, with the trial, in your own way."

"We propose to ask you a few questions, and in your answers you may defend yourself, or admit your guilt. In the first place, did you ever say that you did not believe that God ordained the institution of slavery?"

"I believe that God did not ordain the institution of slavery."

"Did not God command the Israelites to buy slaves from the Canaanitish nations, and to hold them as their property for ever?"

"The Canaanites had filled their cup of iniquity to overflowing, and God commanded the Israelites to exterminate them; this, in violation of God's command, they failed to do. God afterwards permitted the Hebrews to reduce them to a state of servitude; but the punishment visited upon those seven wicked nations by the command of God, does not justify war or the slave-trade."

"Did you say that you were opposed to the slavery which existed in the time of Christ?"

"I did, because the system of slavery prevailing in Christ's day was cruel in the extreme; it conferred the power of life and death upon the master, and was attended with innumerable evils. The slave had the same complexion as his master; and by changing his servile garb for the citizen dress, he could not be recognised as a slave. You yourself profess to be opposed to white slavery."

"Did you state that you believed Paul, when he sent Onesimus back to Philemon, had no idea that he would be regarded as a slave, and treated as such after his return?"

"I did. My proof is in Philemon, verses 15 and 16, where the apostle asks that Onesimus be received, not as a servant, but as a brother beloved?"

"Did you tell Mr. Creath that you knew some negroes who were better, in every respect, than some white men?"

"I said that I knew some negroes who were better classical scholars than any white men I had as yet met with in Choctaw county, and that I had known some who were pre-eminent for virtue and holiness. As to natural rights, I made no comparison; nor did I say anything about superiority or inferiority of race. I also stated my belief in the unity of the races."

"Have you any abolition works in your library, and a poem in your scrap-book, entitled 'The Fugitive Slave,' with this couplet as a refrain,

> 'The hounds are baying on my track;
> Christian, will you send me back?'"

"I have not Mrs. Stowe's nor Helper's work; they are contraband in this region, and I could not get them if I wished. I have many works in my library containing sentiments adverse to the institution of slavery. All the works in common use amongst us, on law, physic, and divinity, all the text-books in our schools—in a word, all the works on every subject read and studied by us, were, almost without exception, written by men opposed to the peculiar institution. I am not alone in this matter."

"Parson, I saw Cowper's works in your library, and Cowper says:

> 'I would not have a slave to fan me when I sleep,
> And tremble when I wake, for all the wealth
> That sinews bought and sold have ever earned.'"

"You have Wesley's writings, and Wesley says that 'Human slavery is the sum of all villany.' You have a work which has this couplet:

> 'Two deep, dark stains, mar all our country's bliss:
> Foul slavery one, and one, loathed drunkenness.'

You have the work of an English writer of high repute, who says, 'Forty years ago, some in England doubted whether slavery were a sin, and regarded adultery as a venial offence; but behold the progress of truth! Who now doubts that he who enslaves his fellow-man is guilty of a fearful crime, and that he who violates the seventh commandment is a great sinner in the sight of God?'"

"You are known to be an adept in Phonography, and you are reported to be a correspondent of an abolition Phonographic journal."

"I understand the science of Phonography, and I am a correspondent of a Phonographic journal, but the journal eschews politics."

Another member of the committee then interrogated me.

"Parson Aughey, what is Funnyography?

"Phonography, sir, is a system of writing by means of a philosophic alphabet, composed of the simplest geometrical signs, in which one mark is used to represent one and invariably the same sound."

"Kin you talk Funnyography? and where does them folks live what talks it?"

"Yes, sir, I converse fluently in Phonography, and those who speak the language live in Columbia."

"In the Destrict?"

"No, sir, in the poetical Columbia."

I was next interrogated by another member of the committee.

"Parson Aughey, is Phonography a Abolition fixin?"

"No, sir; Phonography, abstractly considered, has no political complexion; it may be used to promote either side of any question, sacred or profane, mental, moral, physical, or political."

"Well, you ought to write and talk plain English, what common folks can understand, or we'll have to say of you, what Agrippa said of Paul, 'Much learning hath made thee mad.' Suppose you was to preach in Phonography, who'd understand it?—who'd know what was piped or harped? I'll bet high some Yankee invented it to spread his abolition notions underhandedly. I, for one, would be in favour of makin' the parson promise to write and talk no more in Phonography. I'll bet Phonography is agin slavery, tho' I never hearn tell of it before. I'm agin all secret societies. I'm agin the Odd-fellers, Free-ma-sons, Sons of Temperance, Good Templars and Phonography. I want to know what's writ and what's talked. You can't throw dust in my eyes. Phonography, from what I've found out about it to-day, is agin the Confederate States, and we ought to be agin it."

Parson Locke then resumed:

"I must stop this digression. Parson Aughey, are you in favour of the South?"

"I am in favour of the South, and have always endeavoured to promote the best interests of the South. However, I never deemed it for the best interests of the South to secede. I talked against secession, and voted against secession, because I thought that the best interests of the South would be put in jeopardy by the secession of the Southern States. I was honest in my convictions, and acted accordingly. Could the sacrifice of my life have stayed the swelling tide of secession, it would gladly have been made."

"It is said that you have never prayed for the Southern Confederacy."

"I have prayed for the whole world, though it is true that I have never named the Confederate States in prayer."

"You may retire."

After I had retired, the committee held a long consultation. My answers were not satisfactory. I never learned all that transpired. They brought in no formal verdict. The majority considered me a dangerous man, but feared to take my life, as they were, with one exception, adherents of other denominations, and they knew that my people were devotedly attached to me before the secession movement. Some of the secessionists swore that they would go to my house and murder me, when they learned that the committee had not hanged me. My friends provided me secretly with arms, and I determined to defend myself to the last. I slept with a double-barrelled shot-gun at my head, and was prepared to defend myself against a dozen at least.

Learning that I was not acceptable to many of the members of my church, whilst my life was in continual jeopardy, and my family in a state of constant alarm, I abandoned my field of labour, and sought for safety in a more congenial clime. I intended to go North. Jeff. Davis and his Congress had granted permission to all who so desired, to leave the South. Several Union men of my acquaintance applied for passports, but were refused. The proclamation to grant permits was an act of perfidy; all those, so far as I am informed, who made application for them, were refused. The design in thus acting was to get Union men to declare themselves as such, and afterwards to punish them for their sentiments by forcing them into the army, confining them in prison, shooting them, or lynching them by mob violence. Finding that were I to demand a passport to go north, I would be placed on the proscribed list, and my life endangered still more, I declared my intention of going back to Tishomingo county, in which I owned property, and which was the home of many of my relatives. I knew that I would be safer there, for this county had elected

Union delegates by a majority of over fourteen hundred, and a strong Union sentiment had always prevailed.

On my arrival in Tishomingo, I found that the great heart of the county still beat true to the music of the Union. Being thrown out of employment I deemed it my duty, in every possible way, to sustain the Union cause and the enforcement of the laws. It was impossible to go north. Union sentiments could be expressed with safety in many localities. Corinth, Iuka, and Rienzi had, from the commencement of the war, been camps of instruction for the training of Confederate soldiers. These three towns in the county being thus occupied, Union men found it necessary to be more cautious, as the cavalry frequently made raids through the county, arresting and maltreating those suspected of disaffection. After the reduction of Forts Henry and Donelson, and the surrender of Nashville, the Confederates made the Memphis and Charleston railroad the base of their operations, their armies extending from Memphis to Chattanooga. Soon, however, they were all concentrated at Corinth, a town in Tishomingo county, at the junction of the Memphis and Charleston railroad with the Mobile and Ohio. After the battle of Shiloh, which was fought on the 6th and 7th of April, the Federal troops held their advance at Farmington, four miles from Corinth, while the Confederates occupied Corinth, their rear guard holding Rienzi, twelve miles south, on the Mobile and Ohio railroad.

Thus there were two vast armies encamped in Tishomingo county. Being within the Confederate lines, I, in common with many others, found it difficult to evade the conscript law. Knowing that in a multitude of counsellors there is wisdom, we held secret meetings, in order to devise the best method of resisting the law. We met at night, and had our countersigns to prevent detection. Often our wives, sisters, and daughters met with us. Our meeting-place was some ravine, or secluded glen, as far as possible from the haunts of the secessionists; all were armed; even the ladies had revolvers, and could use them too. The crime of treason we were resolved not to commit. Our counsels were somewhat divided, some advocating, as a matter of policy, the propriety of attending the militia musters, others opposing it for conscience' sake, and for the purpose of avoiding every appearance of evil. Many who would not muster as conscripts, resolved to escape to the Federal lines; and making the attempt two or three at a time, succeeded in crossing the Tennessee river, and reaching the Union army, enlisted under the old flag, and have since done good service as patriot warriors. Some who were willing to muster as conscripts, were impressed into the Confederate service, and I know not whether they ever found an opportunity to desert. Others, myself among the number, were saved by the timely arrival of the Federal troops, and the occupation of the county by them, after Beauregard's evacuation of Corinth. I had received three citations to attend muster, but disregarding them, I was summoned to attend a court-martial on the first day of June, at the house of Mr. Jim Mock. The following is a copy of the citation.

Ma the 22d. 1862

*Parson Awhay*, You havent tended nun of our musttters as a konskrip. Now you is her bi sumenzd to attend a kort marshal on Jun the fust at Jim Mook.

When I received the summons, I resolved to attempt reaching the Union lines at Farmington. Two of my friends, who had received a similar summons, expected to accompany me. On the 29th of May, I left for Rienzi, where my two friends were to meet me. I had not been many hours in Rienzi when it became evident that the Confederates were evacuating Corinth. On the 1st of June, (the day the court-martial was to convene,) I had the pleasure of once more beholding the star-spangled banner as it was borne in front of General Granger's command, which led the van of the pursuing army. Had I remained and attended the court-martial, I would have been forced into the army. Were I then to declare that I would not take up arms against the United States, I would have been shot, as many have been, for their refusal thus to act. General Rosecrans, on his arrival, made his head-quarters at my brother's house, where I had the pleasure of forming his acquaintance, together with that of Generals Smith, Granger, and Pope. As this county was now occupied by the Federal army, I returned to my father-in-law's, within five miles of which place the court martial had been ordered to convene, considering myself comparatively safe. I learned that the court-martial never met, as Colonel Elliott, in his successful raid upon Boonville, had passed Jim Mock's, scaring him to such a degree, that he did not venture to sleep in his house for two weeks. The Union cavalry scoured the country in all directions, daily, and we were rejoicing at the prospect of continuous safety, and freedom from outrage.

The Rebels, during their retreat, had burned all the cotton which was accessible to their cavalry, on their route. At night, the flames of the burning cotton lighted up the horizon for miles around. These baleful pyres, with their lurid glare, bore sad testimony to the horrors of war. In this wanton destruction of the great southern staple, many poor families lost their whole staff of bread, and starvation stared them in the face. Many would have perished, had it not been for the liberal contributions of the North; for, learning the sufferings of the poor of the South, whose whole labour had been destroyed by pretended friends, they sent provisions and money, and thus many who were left in utter destitution, were saved by this timely succor. I have heard the rejoicings of the poor, who, abandoned by their supposed friends, were saved, with their children, from death, by the beneficence of those whom they had been taught to regard as enemies the most bitter, implacable, unmerciful, and persistent. Their prayer may well be, Save us from our friends, whose tender mercies are cruel! I have never known a man to burn his own cotton, but I have heard their bitter anathemas hurled against those who thus robbed them, and their denunciations were loud and deep against the government which authorized such cruelty. It is true that those who thus lose their cotton, if secessionists, receive a "promise to pay," which all regard as not worth the paper on which it is written. Ere pay-day, those who are dependent on their cotton for the necessaries of life, would have passed the bourne whence no traveller returns. 'Tis like the Confederate bonds—at first they were made payable two years after date, and printed upon paper which would be worn out entirely in six months, and would have become illegible in half that time. The succeeding issues were made payable six months after the ratification of a treaty of peace between the United States and the Confederate States. Though not a prophet, nor a prophet's son, I venture the prediction that those bonds will never be due. The war of elements, the wreck of matter, and the crush of worlds, announcing the end of all things, will be heard sooner.

## CHAPTER III.

### ARREST, ESCAPE, AND RECAPTURE.

**High price of Provisions—Holland Lindsay's Family—The arrest—Captain Hill—Appearance before Colonel Bradfute at Fulton—Arrest of Benjamin Clarke—Bradfute's Insolence—General Chalmers—The clerical Spy—General Pfeifer—Under guard—Priceville—General Gordon—Bound for Tupelo—The Prisoners entering the Dungeon—Captain Bruce—Lieutenant Richard Malone—Prison Fare and Treatment—Menial Service—Resolve to escape—Plan of escape—Federal Prisoners—Co-operation of the Prisoners—Declaration of Independence—The Escape—The Separation—Concealment—Travel on the Underground Railroad—Pursuit by Cavalry and Bloodhounds—The Arrest—Dan Barnes, the Mail-robber—Perfidy—Heavily ironed—Return to Tupelo.**

AT this time—May and June, 1862—all marketable commodities were commanding fabulous prices; as a lady declared, it would soon be necessary, on going to a store, to carry two baskets, one to hold the money, and the other the goods purchased. Flour was thirty dollars per barrel, bacon forty cents per pound, and coffee one dollar per pound. Salt was nominally one hundred dollars per sack of one hundred pounds, or one dollar per pound, but there was none to be obtained even at that price. Ladies were compelled to dispense with salt in their culinary operations; even the butter was unsalted. Cotton-cards, an article used in every house at the South, the ordinary price of which is fifty cents per pair, were selling at twenty-five dollars per pair, and wool-cards at fifteen dollars per pair, the usual price being thirty-eight cents. All the cotton used in the manufacture of home-made cloth, is carded into rolls upon these cotton-cards, which are brought from the North, there being not a single manufactory of them in the South. When the supply on hand becomes exhausted, the southern home manufacture of cloth must cease, no one as yet having been able to suggest a substitute for the cotton-card. There are only three factories in Mississippi, which must cease running as soon as their machinery wears out, as the most important parts of the machinery in those factories are supplied from the North. The people are fully aware of these difficulties, but they can devise no remedy, hence the high price of all articles used in the manufacture of all kinds of cloths. All manufactured goods were commanding fabulous prices. On the occupation of the county by Federal troops, goods could be obtained at reasonable prices, but our money was all gone, except Confederate bonds, which were worthless. Planters who were beyond the lines of the retreating army had cotton, but many of them feared to sell it, as the Rebels professed to regard it treason to trade with the invaders, and threatened to execute the penalty in every case. As there was no penalty attached to the selling of cotton by one citizen of Mississippi to another, some of my friends offered to sell me their cotton for a reasonable price.

I was solicited also to act as their agent in the purchase of commodities. I agreed to this risk, because of the urgent need of my friends, many of whom were suffering greatly for the indispensable necessaries of life. I thought it was better that one should suffer, than that the whole people should perish. By this arrangement my Union friends would escape the punishment meted out to those who were found guilty of trading with the Yankees; if discovered, I alone would be amenable to their unjust and cruel law, and they would thus save their cotton, which was liable to be destroyed at any moment by a dash of rebel cavalry. I now hired a large number of wagons to haul cotton into Eastport and Iuka, that I might ship it to the loyal States. On the 2d of June the wagons were to rendezvous at a certain point; there were a sufficient number to haul one hundred bales per trip. I hoped to keep them running for some time.

On the first of June I rode to Mr. Holland Lindsay's on business. I had learned that he was a rabid secessionist, but supposed that no rebel cavalry had come so far north as his house since the evacuation of Corinth. Mr. Lindsay had gone to a neighbour's. His wife was weaving; she was a coarse, masculine woman, and withal possessed of strong prejudice against all whom she did not like, but especially the

Yankees. I sat down to await the arrival of her husband, and it was not long before Mrs. Lindsay broached the exciting topic of the day, the war. She thus vented her spleen against the Yankees.

"There was some Yankee calvary passed here last week—they asked me if there wos ony rebels scoutin round here lately. I jest told em it want none of ther bizness. Them nasty, good for nothin scamps callen our men rebels. Them nigger-stealin, triflin scoundrels. They runs off our niggers, and wont let us take em to Mexico and the other territories."

I ventured to remark, "The Yankees are mean, indeed, not to let *us* take *our* negroes to the Territories, and not to help catch them for *us* when they run off."

The emphatic *us* and *our* nettled her, as none of the Lindsays ever owned a negro, being classed by the southern nabobs as among the *poor white trash;* nor did I ever own a slave. Her husband, however, had once been sent to the Legislature, which led the family to ape the manners, and studiously copy the ultraism of the classes above them. Mrs. Lindsay became morose. I concluded to ride over and see her husband.

On my way I met a member of Hill's cavalry. He halted me, inquired my name and business, which I gave. He said that, years ago, he had heard me preach, and that he was well acquainted with my brothers-in-law, who were officers in the Rebel army. He informed me that his uncle, Mr. Lindsay, had gone across the field home, and that he himself was on his way there. I returned with him, but fearing arrest, my business was hastily attended to, and I at once started for my horse. By this time one or two other cavalry-men rode up. I heard Mrs. Lindsay informing her nephew that I was a Union man, and advising my arrest. When I had reached my horse, Mr. Davis, Lindsay's nephew arrested me, and sent my horse to the stable. After, supper my horse was brought, and I was taken to camp. Four men were detached to guard me during the night. They ordered me to lie down on the ground and sleep. As it had rained during the day, and I had no blanket, I insisted upon going to a Mr. Spigener's, about fifty yards distant, to secure a bed. After some discussion they consented, the guards remaining in the room, and guarding me by turns during the night. The next morning I sought Captain Hill, and asked permission to return home, when the following colloquy ensued.

"Are you a Union man?"

"I voted the Union ticket, sir."

"That is not a fair answer. I voted the Union ticket myself, and am now warring against the Union."

"I have seen no good reason for changing my sentiments."

"You confess, then, that you are a Union man?"

"I do; I regard the union of these States as of paramount importance to the welfare of the people inhabiting them."

"You must go to head-quarters, where you will be dealt with as we are accustomed to deal with all the abettors of an Abolition government."

A heavy guard was then detached to take charge of me; and the company set off for Fulton, the county seat of Ittawamba county, Mississippi, distant thirty miles. After going about ten miles, we halted, and two men were detached to go forward with the prisoners, a Mr. Benjamin Clarke and myself. Our guards were Dr. Crossland, of Burnsville, Tishomingo county, Mississippi, and Ferdinand Woodruff. They were under the influence of liquor, and talked incessantly, cursing and insulting us, on every occasion, by abusive language. They detailed to each other a history of their licentious amours. We halted for dinner at one o'clock, and being out of money, they asked me to pay their bill, which I did, they promising to refund the amount when they reached Fulton. This they forgot to do.

On our arrival at Fulton, we were taken into the office of the commander of the post, Colonel Bradfute. My fellow-prisoner was examined first. Woodruff stated that they had played off on Mr. Clarke—calling on him, as he was plowing in the field, stating that they were Federal soldiers. They asked Clarke what were his political views. He replied that he always had been a Union man—had voted the Union ticket, and would do it again, if another election were held; that he hated the secession principles, and would enlist in the Federal army as soon as he got his crop in such a condition that his family could attend to it. On hearing this statement, Bradfute became very angry, swearing that Clarke ought to be taken out and shot then, but that a few days' respite would make but little difference. Said he, addressing the guards, had you hung Clarke, you would have saved us some trouble, and have done your country good service. The Colonel, turning round, glared upon me with eyes inflamed with passion and liquor, and thus addressed me:

"Are you a Union man too?"

"I am, sir. I have never denied it."

"Where do you reside?"

"I consider Rienzi my home, but have been staying for some time at my father-in-law's, in the south-eastern part of Tishomingo county."

"What is your father-in-law's name?"

"Mr. Alexander Paden."

"I know the old gentleman and his three sons. They are all in the Confederate service. They are brave men, and have done some hard fighting in our cause. How happens it that you look at matters in a different light from your relatives?"

"I am not guided in my opinions by the views of my friends."

"What is your profession?"

"I am a minister of the gospel."

"I suppose, then, that you go to the Bible for your politics, and that you are a sort of higher-law man."

"My Bible teaches, 'Let every soul be subject to the higher powers, for there is no power but of God; the powers that be, are ordained of God. Whosoever, therefore, resisteth the power, resisteth the ordinance of God; and they that resist shall receive to themselves damnation.' I have seen no reason for resistance to the government under which we have, as a nation, so long prospered."

"I command you to hush, sir; you shan't preach treason to me, and if you get your deserts you will be hung immediately. Have you ever been within the Federal lines?"

"I have, sir."

"At what points?"

"At Rienzi and Iuka."

"When were you at Iuka?"

"On last Saturday."

"Had the Federals a large force at that place, and who was in command?"

"They have a large force, and Generals Thomas and Steadman are in command."

"That is contrary to the reports of our scouts, who say that there are but two regiments in the town. I fear you are purposely trying to mislead us."

"General Steadman has but two regiments in the town, but General Thomas is within striking distance with a large force."

"What was your business in Iuka?"

"I went there to pay a debt of fifty dollars which a widow owed, as she wished it to be paid in Confederate money before it became worthless."

"Have you a Federal pass?"

"I have none with me, but have one at home."

"How does it read?"

"It was given by General Nelson, and reads thus: 'The bearer, Rev. John H. Aughey, has permission to pass backward and forward through the lines of this division at will.'"

"Where were you born?"

"I was born in New Hartford, Oneida county, New York."

"Yankee born," said the Colonel, with a sneer; "you deserve death at the rope's-end, aud if I had the power I would hang all Yankees who are among us, for they are all tories, whatever may be their pretensions."

"My being born north of the nigger-line, Colonel, if a crime worthy of death, was certainly not my fault, but the fault of my parents. They did not so much as consult me in regard to any preference I might have concerning the place of my nativity."

Woodruff, one of my guards, now informed the Colonel that I was a spy, and, while the Confederates were at Corinth, had, to his certain knowledge, been three times at Nashville, carrying information. I told Woodruff that his statement was false, and that he knew it; that I had never been at Nashville in my life. General Chalmers, who was present, and Colonel Bradfute, at the conclusion of the examination, spent fifteen or twenty minutes in bitterly cursing all Yankees, tories, and traitors, as they termed us. All the conversation of the rebel officers was interlarded with the most horrid profanity. General Chalmers, in speaking, invariably called me the clerical spy. We were placed under guard, and sent to Brooksville, ten miles distant, the head-quarters of General Pfeifer. Immediately after our arrival, we were soundly berated by General Pfeifer, and then sent out to the camp, half a mile from the town, where we were placed under guard for the night, in a small plot of ground surrounded by a chain.

We had no supper, and no blankets to sleep on. Our bed was the cold ground, our covering the blue canopy of heaven. The next morning we were started, without breakfast, under a heavy guard, numbering fourteen cavalry, to Priceville, six miles west of Brooksville. Priceville was named in honour of General Sterling Price, or rather the little village where he encamped had its name changed in his honour. When we reached Priceville we were taken to the head-quarters of General Jordan, and immediately brought into his presence. After reading the letter handed to him by one of the guard, he said, looking sternly at me,

"You are charged with sedition."

I asked him what sedition meant, to which he replied:

"It means enough to hang you, you villanous tory!"

He also asked me where I was born. My reply was, in the State of New York, near Utica, in Oneida county.

"Then you doubly deserve death," said he.

"As to the guilt of my nativity," said I, "it is not my fault, for I could not have helped it if I had tried. But I glory in my native State. She has never done anything to disgrace her. She never repudiated her just debts, nor committed any other disgraceful act."

"Well, you ought to have staid there, or have gone back when Mississippi seceded."

"Give me an opportunity, and I will go instanter."

"The first *going* you will do, will be to go to hell, where, if the devil had his due, you would have been long ago; and before you leave us, we will give you a free ticket to the shades infernal."

"Thank you for your kind offer to give me a free pass to the infernal regions. I did not know before that you were the devil's ticket-agent. You have me in your power, and may destroy my life; but when you have done that, there is no more that you can do."

Very little was said to my fellow-prisoner, Clarke. A few curses for a traitor, tory, &c., was about all. We were now placed under guard, and conducted to Tupelo, and after visiting the provost-marshal's office and the office of the commander of the post, whose names were Peden and Clare, we were committed to the Central Military Prison. As we entered, Captain Bruce and Lieutenant Malone (two gentlemen who had been elected to those offices by their fellow-prisoners) received us with a cordial greeting. Captain Bruce thus addressed us:

"Welcome, gentlemen, thrice welcome. I am rejoiced to see you at my hotel. We are now doing a land-office business, as the large number of my boarders, whom you see, will testify. We have numerous arrivals daily, whilst the departures are very few, giving evidence that all are satisfied with their treatment. The bill of fare is not very extensive. In these war times we must not expect the luxuries of life, but be content with the necessaries. It is true, we cannot furnish you with coffee, or molasses, or sugar, or salt, or beef, or vegetables; but we have something more substantial—we have flour, rather dark in colour, to be sure, but people must not be squeamish. The boarders are required to do their own cooking, as they could otherwise have but little exercise; we consider it a sanitary measure, exercise being indispensable to health. We furnish the boarders, also, with meat—none of your lean meat, either, but fat middling, with a streak of lean in it. The Bible promises the righteous that their bread shall be given, and their water sure; but we go beyond the promise, and give not only bread (or rather the flour to make it) and water, but also fat, strong meat. What room will you be pleased to have?"

I replied, that as they seemed to be crowded, I would choose number 199.

"Well," said the Captain, "it shall be prepared. Lieutenant Malone, have room number 199 fitted up for the reception of these gentlemen."

Lieutenant Malone replied, that the room designated would be fitted up in style for our reception. He asked us if we had dined.

"No," replied Clarke; "we have not tasted

food since yesterday at noon, when the Parson paid for his own dinner and the dinner of the guards. We asked for something to eat, but were as often refused, and now we are in a starving condition."

"I pity you," said Malone, laying aside his facetious style; "you shall have something to eat as soon as it can be cooked."

He then went to some of the prisoners, and set them to cooking, and we were soon furnished with the best repast the poor fellows could supply.

We entered the prison July 3d, 1862, at two o'clock, P. M. Our prison was a grocery-house, its dimensions about twenty-five by fifty feet. When we were incarcerated, there were about seventy prisoners in the building, whites, mulattoes and negroes. The prison was filthy in the extreme, and filled with vermin; even our food was infested with them. No brooms were furnished us, and we could not sweep the floor. No beds were furnished, and we were compelled to lie upon the floor, with no covering, and nothing but the hard planks beneath us.

Several times a day officers would come in and order a specified number of men to go and work, under a strong guard. We were made to clean the streets, roll barrels, and clean the hospital; but our own prison we were not permitted to clean. Every kind of drudgery, and the most menial services, were imposed upon us.

The crimes charged upon the prisoners were desertion, trading with the Yankees, adhesion to the United States government or Unionism, acting as spies, refusing Confederate bonds, and piloting the Yankees. The crime of the negroes and mulattoes was endeavouring to escape on the underground railroad from Dixie land and the Iron Furnace. These remained till their masters were informed of their arrest, and came for and released them. On the evening preceding our imprisonment, two prisoners had been led out and shot, and I soon learned that this was no unusual occurrence. Nearly every day witnessed the execution of one or more of us. Those who were doomed to die were heavily ironed. In some cases, however, those who were not in fetters were taken out and shot or hanged, often with no previous warning; though sometimes a few hours warning was given.

Our privations were so great from a want of proper food and water—for the scanty amount of water furnished us was tepid and foul—and from a lack of beds, cots, couches, or something better than a filthy floor whereon to sleep, that I resolved to attempt an escape at the risk of my life. I felt confident that I could not long survive such cruel treatment. As soon as my arrest was known to the thirty-second Mississippi regiment, encamped in the suburbs of Tupelo, the colonel, major, adjutant, and one of the captains called upon me. This regiment was raised in Tishomingo county, one of the companies, the Zollicoffer Avengers, being from Rienzi, where I had been for years proprietor and Principal of the Rienzi Female Seminary. The daughters of many of the officers of this regiment had been educated at this Seminary during my superintendence. Some of these officers had expressed themselves under great obligations to me, for the thorough, moral, mental, and physical training of their children while under my care. As proof of this, I have their own statements, as published in the public journals of the day. Owing me a debt of gratitude, as they professed, could I expect less than the manifestation of deep sympathy for me in my sad condition—confined in a gloomy dungeon, deprived of the comforts, yea, even the necessaries of life, menaced and insulted by the officers in whose power I was? Whatever may have been my hopes, they were doomed to be blasted. These summer friends, so obsequious in my prosperity, conversed for a while on indifferent topics, never alluding to my condition, and as I did not obtrude it upon their attention, they left, promising to call again. I said, "Do so, gentlemen; you will always find me *at home*." Adjutant Irion, as he passed out, asked Lieutenant Malone what the charge was against me. Malone replied that I was charged with being a Union man. The adjutant said, in a bitter and sarcastic tone, that I should never have been brought to Tupelo, but on my arrest should have been sent to hell from the lowest limb of the nearest tree.

Having determined to escape at all hazards, I sought out an accomplice, a *compagnon de voyage;* that person was Richard Malone; his piercing eye, his intellectual physiognomy, led me to believe that if he consented to make the attempt with me, our chances for escape would be good. I drew Malone to one side, and covertly introduced the matter. He soon got my idea, and drawing from his pocket a paper, showed me the route mapped out which he intended to pursue, as he had for some days determined to escape, or die in the attempt. He was charged with being a spy, and there was little doubt that they would establish his guilt by false testimony. We went out now under every possible pretext. We no longer shunned the guard who came to obtain prisoners to do servile labour. Our object being to reconnoitre, in order to learn where guards were stationed, and to determine the best method of escape through the town after leaving the prison. During the day we made these observations: that there were two guards stationed at the back door, who were very verdant; that they would, after relief, come on duty again at midnight; that there was a building on the south side of the prison, extending beyond the prison and beyond the guards; that the moon would set about eleven o'clock, P. M.; that there were no guards stationed on the south side of the prison during the day; that one of the planks in the floor could be easily removed; and that there were several holes, when we were once under the floor, by which egress might be made either on the north or south side; that the coast was probably clearest in the direction of a corn-field some two hundred yards distant in a northwest direction.

At four o'clock P. M., our plan was fully matured. At midnight, (the moon being down, and the verdant guards on duty) we would raise the plank, get under the floor, and myself in the advance, make our exit through one of the holes on the south side of the jail, then crawl to the building, some fifteen feet distant, and continue crawling till we passed the guards; then rise and make our way as cautiously as possible, to a point in the corn-field, a short distance in the rear of a garment which was hanging upon the fence. The one who first arrived must await the other. A signal was agreed upon, to prevent mistake. If the guards ordered us to halt, we had resolved to risk their fire, our watchword being, Liberty or death!

About this time the prisoners chose me their chaplain by acclamation. During the day, we made known our intention of escaping to several fellow-prisoners, who promised us all the assistance in their power. All the prisoners who knew of the matter, earnestly desired our escape, and co-operated with us in effecting it. Clarke and Robinson begged us to take them along, averring there was no doubt that they would be shot. Malone told them that no more than two could go together; that if they wished to escape, they could make the attempt half an hour after us, which they agreed to. Clarke, however, came to me, and desired me to take him along, as he would rather go with us than with Robinson. He had a wife and five small children dependent on him for support, and if he perished, they must perish too. I consulted Malone, but he would not agree to have Clarke go with us. Three would be too many for safety, and he doubted whether Clarke had sufficient nerve to face the glittering bayonet, or tact enough to pass through the camps without detection. He might commit some blunder which would endanger our safety. I informed Clarke that the arrangement made, in which he and Robinson were to go together, must be adhered to. He begged me, by all that was sacred, to take him along. But Malone was inexorable, and I thought it best to acquiesce in his judgment.

Night drew on apace. Thick darkness gathered around us, and murky clouds covered the sky, as we sat down with the Federal prisoners to our scanty allowance. While partaking of our rude fare, Malone thus spoke:

"This day is the 4th of July, 1862, the anniversary of our patriot fathers' declaration of independence of British tyranny and oppression. They had much to complain of. They suffered grievous wrongs and cruel bondage. But eighty-six years ago to-day they declared themselves to be a free and independent people, who would rather die than be again enslaved. Of what worth was their declaration if they had remained inactive? Supineness would not have saved them. But trusting in our God, who gives success to the righteous cause, they imperilled their lives, they hazarded their fortunes, and with untiring energy and sleepless vigilance they contested to the bitter end against all efforts to deprive them of their inalienable rights. Success crowned their efforts, and they rid themselves of tyrants' chains. We (I allude to my friend, Parson Aughey, and myself,) degenerate sons of these noble sires, have suffered wrong, nay, gross outrage. Citizens of the sunny South, guilty of no offence whatever, not even of constructive crime, we are immured in a loathsome dungeon, deprived of the comforts of life, separated from our families, and suffered to have no communication with them; dragging out a miserable existence, which an ignominious death on the scaffold must soon end. We, therefore, John H. Aughey and Richard Malone, in view of these accumulated wrongs and outrages, solemnly swear before High Heaven, and in presence of these witnesses, that we will be free, or perish in the attempt. Appealing to the God of liberty, of truth, and of righteousness, for the rectitude of our motives and the justness of our cause, we commit ourselves into his hands, and implore his protection amid the dangers through which we are about to pass, and humbly pray that he will give us success, and restore us speedily to our families and friends, and to the enjoyment of our inalienable rights, life, liberty, and the pursuit of happiness."

Grasping the Lieutenant by the hand, I consented to this Declaration of Independence of rebel thraldom. We gave our respective addresses to our friends, who promised, that if they were ever liberated, and we were killed by the guards, they would write to our families, informing them of the manner of our death.

About ten o'clock, Malone raised the plank, and I went under to reconnoitre. I remained under the floor about ten minutes, having learned that there were no guards patroling the south side of the house, as we feared might be the case after night. We had learned, from observation, that there were none during the day. Just at the noon of night, we heard the relief called. Malone and I endeavoured to find the prisoners who were to raise the plank, but not being able readily to do so, we raised the plank ourselves, and both got under without difficulty. Malone getting under first, was, contrary to agreement, compelled to take the lead. As he was passing out, he made considerable noise. To warn him of the danger, I patted him on the back. Reaching back, he gave my hand a warm pressure, to assure me that all was right, and passed out. I followed, and reached the designated point in the cornfield in about half an hour, having to use the utmost precaution, and in some cases to pass the guards by crawling in a serpentine manner. When I arrived, I gave the preconcerted signal, but Malone was nowhere to be seen. I waited for him two hours at least, when I was compelled to seek my safety alone.

Not being able to meet with my friend, I regarded as a great misfortune, because, after reaching a point ten miles north of Tupelo, he would be familiar with the country. I had frequently passed through the town on the railroad, but knew nothing of the country through which I must travel. Somewhat depressed in spirits at the loss of my *compagnon de voyage*, I resolved to reach my family by the safest and most practicable route. Still in the midst of camps, I had considerable difficulty in making my way out of them. When I thought that this had been effected, I found that day was brightening in the east. Looking around for some place to hide, I soon found a dense, though small thicket, in which I secreted myself as covertly as possible. Having slept but little since my arrest, I endeavoured to compose myself to slumber, and partially succeded; but soon the noise and confusion of soldiers passing and re-passing near, awoke and alarmed me. I soon learned that I was near a camp, and that the soldiers had found a suitable place for bathing in a creek which ran within thirty yards of my place of concealment. There were two paths by which they reached the creek. On one, they passed within fifteen feet of me; on the other, within six or seven. About nine o'clock, I heard the booming of cannon all around me, proceeding from the different camps. The soldiers who passed me stated, in their conversation, that the cannon were firing in honour of a great victory obtained over General McClellan, in Virginia. According to their statement, his whole army, after a succession of losses, during eight days' fighting, had been completely annihilated, and that Stonewall Jackson would be in Washington city before the close of the week.

The day passed slowly away. At one time two soldiers came within a few feet of me in search of blackberries, but passed out without detecting me. At another time two soldiers sat down to converse, so near that their lowest tones were distinctly audible. One informed the other that he had been in town in the morning, and had learned that the *Clerical Spy,* Parson Aughey, and a fellow by the name of Malone, had broke jail, but that they would soon be brought in, as a company of cavalry had been put on their track, with a pack of bloodhounds. Soon after this, one of them arose and struck a bush several times, which seemed to be but a very short distance above my head. I thought that he had discovered me, and was about to rise and run, when I heard him say to his companion, that he had attempted to kill a very large snake, which had escaped to the bushes. I began to feel somewhat uncomfortably situated when I learned that I was in close proximity to a large snake, though I would have preferred meeting with an anaconda, boa-constrictor, rattlesnake, or even the deadly cobra di capello, rather than with those vile secessionists thirsting for innocent blood.

I thought this 5th of July was the longest day I had ever known. The sun was so long in reaching the zenith, and so slow in passing down the steep ecliptic way to the occident. The twilight, too, seemed of endless duration. But as all long days have had an end, so had this. The stars came glittering one by one. I soon recognised that old staunch and immovable friend of all travellers on the underground railroad, the polar-star.

Rising from my lair, I was soon homeward bound, guided by the north-star and an oriental constellation. Plunging into a dense wood I found my rapid advance impeded by the undergrowth, and great difficulty in following my guiding stars, as the boughs of the great oaks rendered them invisible, or dimly seen. Fatigued, hungry, and sleepy, I at length lay down at the foot of a large swamp-oak tree, intending to take a nap, and then rise and pursue my journey. When I awoke the sun was just rising. I arose filled with regret for the time I had lost. Though somewhat refreshed by my sound sleep, yet I was very hungry and almost famished with thirst.

After travelling about half a mile I came to a small log-house on a road-side. Feeling sick and faint, I resolved to go to the house to obtain water, and, if I liked the appearance of the inmates, to reveal my condition, and ask for aid. Upon reaching the house I met the proprietor, but did not like his physiognomy. He looked the villain; a sinister expression, a countenance revealing no intellectuality, except a sort of low cunning, bore testimony that it would be foolish to repose confidence in the possessor of such villanous looks. I asked for water, intending to drink and leave. He pointed to the bucket; I drank and bade him good morning, and turned to leave. I had proceeded but a few steps, when I was ordered, in a stentorian tone, to halt. On looking round, I saw a soldier within a few steps, presenting a double-barrelled gun; another soldier was standing near, heavily armed. I asked by what authority he halted me. To which he replied:

"I know you, sir; I have heard you preach frequently. You are Parson Aughey, and you were arrested and confined in prison at Tupelo. I was in Lowrey's regiment yesterday, and learned that you had broken jail; and now, sir, you must return. My name is Dan Barnes. You may have heard of me."

I had indeed heard of him. He had been guilty of robbing the United States mail, had fled to Napoleon or Helena, Arkansas, where he was arrested, brought back, and incarcerated in jail at Pontotoc, and confined there for nearly a year. As the evidence against him was positive, he would have been sent to the penitentiary; but, fortunately for him, at this juncture Mississippi seceded. There being then no United States officers to execute the laws, he was liberated, and soon after joined the army.

After breakfast, which I paid for, Barnes called me to one side, and told me that he felt sorry for me, and would afford me an opportunity of escaping, if I would pay him a reasonable sum. He had been in a tight place himself, and would have been glad had some friend been near to aid him. He named two hundred and forty dollars as the *reasonable sum* for permitting me to escape. After getting my money, their horses were saddled, and telling me he was playing-off on me, said I must go to General Jordan's head-quarters at Priceville, to which place he and Huff, the proprietor of the log cabin, conducted me.

On my arrival, General Jordan ordered me to be put in irons, and placed under guard. I was taken to a blacksmith's shop in the town, the General accompanying the guard, and heavy iron bands were put around my ankles, and connected by a chain. The bands were put on hot, and my boots were burnt in the operation. The blacksmith seemed averse to the order, and only obeyed it upon compulsion. The General stood by, and saw that it was well done. "Iron him securely—securely, sir," was his oft repeated order. The ironing caused me much

"I was taken to a blacksmith's shop, and heavy iron bands put around my ankles." Page 104.

pain. My ankles were long discoloured from the effects of it.

After my manacles were put on, I was taken back to Tupelo by Barnes and another guard. On my arrival, the commander of the post and the Provost Marshal were filled with joy. Barnes gave them the history of the arrest, stating that I had attempted to bribe him; that he listened to my proposition with indignation, and when he had got the money, performed what he regarded his duty. The commander replied that all the property of traitors was theirs, and that he did right in deceiving me, after accepting the bribe. He also recommended Barnes for promotion for his heroic and patriotic act in arresting me. (Perhaps it secured for him a captaincy.) The following colloquy now took place between the commander of the post, the Provost Marshal, and myself:

"Why did you attempt to leave us?"

"Because, sir, your prison was so filthy, and your fare so meagre and unwholesome, that I could not endure it long, and live."

"Parson, you know the Bible says, the wicked flee when no man pursueth, but the righteous are as bold as a lion. You must have been guilty of crime, or you would not have tried to escape."

"I may have been guilty of the offence charged against me, and yet innocent of real *guilt.*"

"You shall never be taken back to the prison you left, rest assured of that. Did any of the prisoners know of or aid you in your escape?"

"No, sir; none of them knew anything about it."

"Are you telling the truth?"

"I am."

"Where is Malone?"

"I never saw him after I left the building."

"He cannot escape; the cavalry are after him, and he will be brought in soon, dead or alive."

"Why did you attempt to bribe Barnes?"

"It was his own offer. I knew that his cupidity was great, and thought it no harm to accept his offer. If Barnes had his deserts, he would now be hard at work in the penitentiary."

"Did the jury that tried him, acquit him?"

"No. The secession of Mississippi saved him. I refer you to Colonel Tison, who is in Tupelo, for the particulars. He being marshal of North Mississippi, arrested Barnes, and knows all about it. He found on his person the evidence of his guilt, the money and checks stolen when he robbed the mail."

"Parson, you will not be immediately executed, but you will, without doubt, hang in a week or two, so that, if you have any word to send your family, you have permission to do so."

"May I write a letter to my wife?"

"You may, and I will see that it is forwarded to her."

I sat down and wrote a letter, a very common-place letter, to my wife, inserting, occasionally, a word in phonography, which, taken in connection, read thus: "If possible, inform General Rosecrans or Nelson of my arrest." While inspecting the letter, Lieutenant Peden noticed the phonography, and asked me to read it. I read it thus: "My dear wife, I hope to be at home soon. Do not grieve." This letter they never sent. It was merely an act of duplicity on their part, to obtain some concession, which might be used against me. The guard, receiving orders, now conducted me to a hotel, and placed me in a small room, two guards remaining inside, and two at the door outside, with orders to shoot me if I made the least attempt at escape. I remained in this room only a few hours, after which I was taken to my old prison. As I entered, my old friends, the prisoners, crowded around me, and Captain Bruce addressed me in his facetious manner. In prison, his wit had beguiled many a tedious hour. His humour was the pure Attic salt.

"Parson Aughey, you are welcome back to my house, though you have played us rather a scurvy trick in leaving without giving me the least inkling of the matter, or settling your bill."

I replied: "Captain, it was hardly right; but I did not like your fare, and your beds were filled with vermin."

"Well, you do not seem to have fared better since you left, for you have returned."

"Captain, my return is the result of coercion. Some who oppose this principle when applied to themselves, have no scruples in enforcing it upon others.

> "No rogue e'er felt the halter draw,
> With good opinion of the law;"

is an old saw, and the truth of proverbs is seldom affected by time. I am your guest upon compulsion; but remember, I will leave you the first opportunity."

Upon hearing this, an officer present swore that when I again left that building, it would be to cross the railroad, (the place of execution.)

The prisoners gathered around me, and I related to them my adventures. They then informed me of what had transpired during my absence. Clarke was taken out of prison to guide a cavalry company in search of me.

Clarke informed me that they scoured the country, and then went to my father-in-law's; and after searching the premises, returned, believing that I had gone due north towards Rienzi, in which direction another company had been despatched. On their return, Clarke was remanded to jail. At roll-call—seven o'clock, A. M., we were missed. The cavalry were immediately sent in pursuit. All the guards on duty during the night were put under arrest. Our method of escape was soon discovered, and the guards were released, as they were not at fault. A large number of spikes were hammered in the floor, the guards were doubled, and greater vigilance enjoined. The prisoners were questioned, strictly and individually, to learn whether any of them knew of our intention to escape, or had rendered us any assistance. They all positively denied any knowledge of the matter. They asked me whether I had given the officers any information about their knowledge of our designs, and coöperation in effecting them. I replied that I had positively denied that any except Malone and myself were privy to our plans.

I may state here that it is difficult to justify a falsehood. We ought to utter truth always, without exaggeration or prevarication, leaving consequences with God. We should do right without regard to results, for with consequences we have no business; but in this case the temptation to utter an untruth was great. These wicked men, thirsting for my blood, had no right to make me criminate myself or my coadjutors. It would have been wrong for me to give them the information they desired. Truth is too precious for a secessionist, thirsting for innocent blood. Had I refused to answer, they would have suspected that some of my fellow-prisoners aided us, and would have either forced me to tell who they were, or would have hanged me instantly for my refusal. If I had given information, and criminated those who had befriended us, they would have been severely punished, and I have been guilty of the basest ingratitude; I would have been shunned by the prisoners, and regarded as one of the meanest of men, one of the veriest wretches in existence; I could never again ask nor expect aid in a similar attempt to save myself from a violent death.

# CHAPTER IV.

## LIFE IN A DUNGEON.

**Parson Aughey as Chaplain—Description of the Prisoners—Colonel Walter, the Judge Advocate—Charges and Specifications against Parson Aughey—A Citizen of the Confederate States—Execution of two Tennesseeans—Enlistment of Union Prisoners—Colonel Walter's second visit—Day of Execution specified—Farewell Letter to my Wife—Parson Aughey's Obituary penned by himself—Address to his Soul—The Soul's Reply—Farewell Letter to his Parents—The Union Prisoners' Petition to Hon. W. H. Seward—The two Prisoners and the Oath of Allegiance—Irish Stories.**

I WAS remanded to jail on Sabbath, the 6th of July, 1862. On the day of my escape I had been elected chaplain. Captain Bruce asked permission for me to hold divine service, to which no special objection was made. I conducted the services as I would have done were I in my own pulpit. The best order was maintained by the prisoners, and a deep seriousness prevailed. The songs of Zion resounded through the prison-house, and a great concourse of soldiers assembled outside the guards in front of the door, causing considerable interruption by their noise and insulting language. Several officers, also, saw fit to come in and interrupt the services by conversing in a loud tone, and asking me how I liked my jewelry, referring to my fetters. The prisoners protested against their rude and ungentlemanly conduct, but with little effect. They sent a remonstrance to the commander of the post, but he treated it with silent contempt.

As the prisoners insisted upon it, I persisted in preaching, notwithstanding the persecutions endured, as long as I remained with them. We were a motley assemblage. Some were dressed in cloth of finest texture; others were clad in filthy rags. There were present the learned and the illiterate, the rowdy and the minister of the gospel, the holy and the profane, the saint and the sinner. All the Southern States, and every prominent religious denomination were represented. The youth in his nonage, and the gray-haired and very aged man were there. The superior and the subordinate were with us. The descendants of Shem, Ham, and Japheth, were here on the same common level, for in our prison were Afric's dark-browed sons, the descendants of Pocahontas, and the pure Circassian. Death is said to be THE great leveller; the dungeon at Tupelo was *a* great leveller. A fellow-feeling made us wondrous kind; none shared his morsel alone, and a deep and abiding sympathy for each other's woes pervaded every bosom. When our fellow-prisoners were called to die, and were led through us with pallid brows, and agony depicted on their countenances, our expressions of sorrow and commiseration were not loud (through fear) but deep.

On Monday morning an officer entered; my name was called, and I arose from the floor on which I had been reclining. I recognised him as my old friend, Colonel H. W. Walter, of Holly Springs, Mississippi. After the ordinary salutations, he informed me that he was Judge Advocate, and that my trial would take place in a few days, and inquired whether I wished to summon any witnesses. I gave him the names and residences of several witnesses, but he refused to send for them, upon the plea that they were too near the Federal lines, and their cavalry might be in danger of capture were they to proceed thither. I told him that the cavalry which went in pursuit of me had visited that locality. He then wished to know what I desired to prove by those witnesses. I replied that I wished to prove that the specifications in the charge of being a spy were false.

"Your own admissions are sufficient to cause you to lose your life," said the Colonel, "and I will not send for those witnesses."

I replied: "I know that I must die, and you need not go through the formality of a trial. If condemned as a spy, I must be hanged. I only wished the witnesses to prove that Woodruff is a man of no moral worth, that his testimony is false; that Barnes is a mail-robber, and that his testimony, therefore, should be rejected. Proving these facts, the other charges which I admit, will cause me to be shot. I hope I am prepared to die, but do not wish to die a dog's death. Promise me that I shall be shot, and not hanged, and I will cavil no more."

"Parson Aughey, your chances for living are very slender. The proof against you on both charges will be established; the testimony as to your guilt is positive, and spies are always hanged."

He then stated the charges and specifications against me as follows:

First charge—*Treason.*

Specification 1st. That said Aughey stated to a member of Hill's cavalry, that if McClellan were defeated, the North could raise a much larger army in a very short time; that the North would eventually conquer the South, and that he was a Union man—this for the purpose of giving aid and comfort to the enemy.

Specification 2d. That when said Aughey was requested to take the oath of allegiance to the Confederate States, he refused, giving as a reason, that England, France, and himself, had not yet recognised the Southern Confederacy, stating, also, that he had voluntarily taken the oath of allegiance to the United States Government, which he regarded as binding—this in North Mississippi.

Specification 3d. That said Aughey was acting as a Federal agent in the purchase of cotton, and had received from the United States Government a large amount of gold, to pay for the cotton purchased.

Second charge—*Acting as a spy.*

Specification 1st. That said Aughey, while a citizen of the Confederate States, repeatedly came into our lines for the purpose of obtaining information for the benefit of the enemy, and that he passed through the lines of the enemy at pleasure, holding an unlimited pass from General Nelson, granting that privilege—this in the vicinity of Corinth, Mississippi.

Witnesses, —— Wallace, Dan Barnes, Ferdinand Woodruff, —— Williams, David Huff.

I demanded a copy of the charges, which Colonel Walter promised to furnish.

About three o'clock in the afternoon, I went to a couple of prisoners who were heavily ironed; they were handcuffed, had a chain on their legs similar to mine, and were chained together to a post, or to some fixture at the side of the jail. I inquired for what offence they were incarcerated.

The prisoner whom I addressed was a tall gentleman, with a very intellectual countenance, and of prepossessing manners. He was somewhat pale, and wore a sad countenance. He replied:

"We are charged with desertion."

"Did you desert?"

"I enlisted in the Confederate service for twelve months. At the expiration of my term of service, I asked permission to return home, stating that my family were suffering for the necessaries of life; that they lived in Tennessee, which is occupied by Federal troops. Confederate bonds are there not worth the paper on which they are printed; provisions are scarce, and my family have not the means of purchasing. I wish to relieve their wants, and as my term of service has expired, I wish a discharge. This they refused, stating that the Confederate Congress had passed a law requiring all troops who had enlisted for any term, however short, to be held to service during the war, and all who left before that time would be considered guilty of desertion, and if arrested, would be shot. I attempted to return to my family, regarding the law a tyrannical enactment. I was arrested and committed to this prison."

"What will be your fate?"

"I know not, but fear the worst."

I learned that the other prisoner had about the same statement to make, and was also in dread of capital punishment. I left them and walked to the opposite side of the prison, when I observed a file of soldiers drawn up in front of the building. Two officers entered, and walking up to the two prisoners whom I had just left, unfastened their chains, and ordered them to follow. One of the prisoners asked whether he should bring his blanket. "No," replied the officer, in a jocular tone; "you have no more need for a blanket in this world."

On reaching the door, the soldiers separated, received the prisoners in their midst, closed up, and marching them across the railroad, shot them. As the officers passed Captain Bruce, he asked where the prisoners were going. They replied, "Going to be shot!" and showed him the warrant for their execution, having written across it, in red letters, "*Condemned to death!*"

Thus was perpetrated an act of cruel tyranny, which cries loudly to Heaven for vengeance. Two families, helpless and destitute, were thus each deprived of its head, on whom they were dependent for support, and abandoned to the cold charity of a selfish world. The wages they earned by a year's faithful service in behalf of the wicked, cruel, and vindictive Confederate States, was an ignominious death and a dishonoured grave. Will not God visit for this? The widow and the fatherless cry to Heaven for vengeance, and their cries have entered into the ears of the Lord of Sabaoth.

On Tuesday morning, six young men, who had been arrested for their Union sentiments, resolved to escape. Their plan was to enlist in the Confederate service, then to desert on the first opportunity, and make their way to the Federal lines. They consulted me as to the propriety of taking the oath of allegiance under these circumstances. Such a step would give them another chance for life; but were they to profess adherence to their Union principles, they had no hope of living many days. If permitted to enlist, they thought there was little doubt of their escape in a few days; and should a battle take place, no Federal soldiers would be injured by them, and an opportunity to desert might occur during the engagement. I drew up a paper for them, requesting permission to enlist in a company which they specified. Their petition was granted by the authorities, and they were removed from prison to the camp. I feel confident that ere this, they are safe in the Federal lines, for they knew the whole country, so as to be able to travel by night or by day, with little danger of detection. They had all been arrested at their homes by the Rebel cavalry. They were bitter in sentiiment against the military usurpation, self-styled the Confederate States of America.

This (Tuesday) evening, Colonel Walter called again, to give me a copy of the charges against me. He informed me that my trial had been deferred till Monday, the 15th inst. He also informed me in advance, that I must die, and that, doubtless, on the day after the trial. I asked and obtained permission to send for the Rev. Dr. Lyon, of Columbus, Mississippi, to be present at my execution. Dr. Lyon and I were co-presbyters, both being members of the Tombeckbee Presbytery. Colonel Walter was a renegade Yankee. Coming from Michigan to Mississippi, he married the daughter of a wealthy slave-holder. Obtaining through her the control of a large number of slaves, he became a very ultra advocate of the peculiar institution, and a rabid secessionist.

Soon after Colonel Walter left, Colonel Ware came in, and asked me if I had been President of a Female College in Rienzi. I replied in the affirmative. 'Tis strange, said he, that one who has been so favoured, and one who has accumulated property in the South, should prove a traitor to the land of his adoption, and side with his enemies. I replied that I had given a fair equivalent for every dollar I had obtained from the citizens of the South; that for eleven years I had laboured faithfully as a teacher and minister of the gospel to promote the educational and spiritual interests of the Southern people; and that now I was receiving my reward in being chained, starved, and insulted; and that they intended soon to pay the last instalment by putting me to death ignominiously on the scaffold; I also denied being an enemy to the South. I regarded those who imperilled all her best interests, and plunged her into a protracted and desolating war, as the real enemies of the South. If my advice had been followed, the South and the whole country would now be enjoying its wonted peace and prosperity. He only replied with cursing and vituperation.

Believing my end to be near, I sat down upon the floor of my dungeon, and penned the following letter to my wife.

TUPELO MILITARY DUNGEON, July 10th, 1862.

MY DEAR MARY—The Confederate authorities announce to me that I have only a few more days to live. When you receive this letter, the hand that penned it will be cold in death. My soul will have passed the solemn test before the bar of God; I have a good hope through grace that I will be then rejoicing amid the sacramental host of God's elect, singing the new song of redeeming love in the presence of Him who is the Chief among ten thousand, and the one altogether lovely. Mary, meet me in heaven, where sorrow, and crying, and sin are not known, and where the wicked cease from troubling, and the weary are at rest. I will request your brother Ramsey, and cousin, Captain Tankersley, to convey my body to you. Bury me in the graveyard at Bethany. Plant an evergreen—a cedar—at my head, and one at my feet, and there let me repose in peace, till the Archangel's trump shall sound, calling the dead to the judgment of the great day, and vouchsafing to saints the long wished-for "redemption of the body."

As to my property, it has all been confiscated; and after years of incessant toil, I leave you penniless and dependent; but trust in God. To his protecting care I commit you and our dear little Kate, who has promised that he will be the widow's husband, and the father of the fatherless. Rest assured, the Lord will provide. Only trust in him, and love him with your whole heart, and soul, and mind, and strength. "I know that it shall be well with those that love God." Be not faithless, but believing, and though clouds and thick darkness surround you at present, a more auspicious day will dawn, and God will bring you safely to your journey's end, and our reunion in heaven will be sweet.

Our dear little daughter, Kate, bring up in the nurture and admonition of the Lord. Teach her to walk in wisdom's ways, for her ways are ways of pleasantness, and all her paths are peace. Her mind may be compared to wax, in its susceptibility for receiving impressions, and to marble, for its power of retaining those impressions. O that she may be satisfied early with the mercy of God, that she may rejoice and be glad all her days! Teach her to remember her Creator in the days of her youth, before the evil days come, in which she shall say, I have no pleasure in thee. Make the Bible her constant study, and let its words be as household words to her. Inspire her mind with a reverence for *the Book* which is able to make wise unto salvation. See to it that the words of Christ dwell richly in her soul, that she may be filled with wisdom, and knowledge, and spiritual understanding. Pray for the Holy Spirit to bless your labours and instructions, without which all your efforts would be in vain, and pray that the Third Person of the adorable Trinity may take up his abode in her heart, and dwell with her for ever.

As my duties in regard to instructing our child, will devolve solely on you, take for your guidance, in this respect, Deut. vi. 5—9. Let your example be such as you would wish her to follow. Children are much more inclined to follow example than precept. Exercise care in this respect, for, "as is the mother, so is her daughter."

I regret my family will, from the force of circumstances, be compelled to remain in a land where my death will be considered disgraceful, but it cannot be avoided. The time may come when, even in Mississippi, I may be regarded as a patriot martyr. My conscience is void of offence, as regards the guilt attached to the charges made against me. I am charged with treason against the Confederate States. The charge and the specifications are true, except that I was not a Federal agent in the purchase of cotton. That was a private arrangement altogether. I am also charged with acting as a spy. The specifications under this charge are false. I think that this accusation was made to prevent retaliation by the Federal generals; and in the Rebel army they are not at a loss to prove any charge, however false. Ferdinand Woodruff is their tool to prove me a spy, and he will do it, though he knows his testimony to be as false as that of the suborned witnesses who bore testimony against the Saviour.

How long shall the wicked triumph? How long will God forbear to execute that vengeance which is his, and which he will repay sooner or later! I feel confident that the right cause will prevail, and though I will not live to see it, for my days are numbered, yet I firmly believe that the rebel power will be destroyed utterly.

> "Truth, crushed to earth, will rise again;
> The eternal years of God are hers;
> But error, wounded, writhes in pain,
> And dies amid her worshippers."

I write this letter amid the din and confusion incident to a large number of men crowded into a narrow compass, and free from all restraint. This letter will be transmitted to you by friends. The names of those friends you will know hereafter. They will present your case to General Rosecrans or Nelson, who may obtain a pension for you. My services heretofore in the Union cause are known to them, and I think they will see that you do not suffer; all my real estate will be restored to you if the Union cause triumphs, and I think there is no doubt as to its success. Give my love to all my friends. Remember that I have prayed for you unceasingly during my imprisonment, and my last utterances on earth will be prayers for your welfare.

Farewell. God bless you, and preserve you and our dear little Kate.

Your affectionate husband,

JOHN H. AUGHEY.

I next wrote my obituary, which I placed in the hands of a Union soldier who expected soon to be exchanged. By him it was to be sent to the editors of *The Presbyterian*, published in Philadelphia, with a request that it should appear in their columns.

OBITUARY.

Died, in Tupelo, Ittawamba county, Mississippi, July —, 1862, the Rev. John H. Aughey. The subject of the above notice was executed on the gallows, by authority of the Confederate States, on the charges of treason and acting as a spy.

John H. Aughey was born in New Hartford, Oneida county, New York, May 8th, 1828; removed with his parents to Steubenville, Ohio, in 1837; is an alumnus of Franklin College, New Athens, Harrison county, Ohio; studied theology in Memphis, Tennessee, under the Rev. John H. Gray, D. D., President of Memphis Synodical College—also under the care of the Rev. S. I. Reid of Holly Springs, Mississippi; was licensed to preach the gospel by the Presbytery of Chickasaw, October 4th, 1856; was ordained to the full work of the gospel ministry by the Presbytery of Tombeckbee, at its session in Winston county, Mississippi, in April, 1861. God blessed his labours by giving him many seals to his ministry. After labouring eleven years in the South as a teacher and minister of the gospel, having never injured a citizen of the South either in person or property, he suffered a felon's death for attachment to the Federal Union, because he would not turn traitor to the government which had never in a single instance oppressed, but had always afforded him protection. He rests in peace, and in the hope of a blessed immortality.

> "Leaves have their time to fall,
> And flowers to wither in the north wind's breath,
> And stars to set; but all—
> Thou hast all seasons for thine own, O Death!"

### ADDRESS TO MY SOUL.

O my soul! thou art about to appear in the presence of thy Creator, who is infinite, eternal, unchangeable in his being, power, wisdom, holiness, justice, goodness, and truth. He cannot look upon sin. He is a sin-avenging God, and thou art stained with sin. Thy transgressions are as numerous as the stars of heaven, and the sand that is upon the sea-shore. Thou art totally debased by sin, and thy iniquities abound. Thou art guilty of sins of omission and of commission. Justice would consign thee to everlasting burnings, to dwell with devouring fire, even to everlasting destruction from the presence of the Lord and the glory of his power. Guilty, helpless, wretched as thou art, what is thy plea why sentence of eternal death should not be pronounced against thee?

### THE SOUL'S REPLY.

I plead the merits of the Lord Jesus Christ, whose blood cleanses from *all* sin, even from sins of the deepest dye. I plead the sufferings of Him who bore my sins in his own body, on the tree, and wrought out a perfect righteousness, which I may obtain by simple faith. No money, no price is demanded. This I could not pay, for all my righteousness is as filthy rags, and I must perish, were any part of the price demanded. Nothing in my hand I bring. My salvation must be *all* of grace, or to me it would be hopeless. I trust that Christ will clothe me in the spotless robes of his own righteousness, and present me faultless before his Father. With this trust, I go to the judgment-seat, assured that the soul which trusts in Christ shall never be put to shame. God is faithful who has promised.

MILITARY DUNGEON, Tupelo,
Ittawamba Co., Miss., July 11th, 1862.

DEAR PARENTS—"Life is sweet, and it is a pleasant thing to behold the sun." "All that a man hath, will he give for his life." "Having promise of the life that now is." "The life is more than meat." "They hunt for the *precious* life." The above quotations from the Word of Life, show the high estimate that is placed upon life. My life is not "*precious*" in the eyes of the Secessionists, for their authorities declare that "my chances for living long are extremely slender." "Yet a few days, and me the all-beholding sun shall see no more in all his course." Mourn not for me, my dear parents, as those who have no hope. "For me to live, is Christ; but to die, is gain." I fear not those who, when they have killed the body, have no more that they can do. But I fear Him whose fear casteth out every other fear. When these lines are read by you, their author will be an inhabitant of the Celestial City, the New Jerusalem, and will be reposing in Abraham's bosom, in the midst of the Paradise of God. Next to God, my thanks are due to you, for guiding my infant feet in the paths of wisdom and virtue. In riper years, by precept, I have been warned and instructed. By example I have been led, until my habits were fixed, and then, accompanied by your parental blessing, I sought a distant home, to engage in the arduous duties of life. Whatever success I have met with, whatever influence for good I may have exerted, are all due to your pious training. I owe you a debt of gratitude which I can never repay. Though I cannot, God will grant you a reward lasting as eternity. It will add to that exceeding and eternal weight of glory which will be conferred on you in that day when the heavens shall be dissolved, and the elements melt with fervent heat. I die for my loyalty to the Federal Government. I know that you would not have me turn traitor to save my life. Life is precious, but death, even death on the scaffold, is preferable to dishonour. Remember me kindly to all my friends. Tell sisters Sallie, Mary, and Emma, to meet me in heaven. I know that *my* Redeemer liveth. Dying is but going home. I have taught many how to live, and now I am called to teach them how to die. May God grant that as my day is, so may my strength be, and that, in my last moments, I may not bring dishonour upon my Master's cause, but may glorify him in the fires!

My dear parents, farewell till we meet beyond the river.

Your affectionate son,

JOHN H. AUGHEY.

To DAVID and ELIZABETH AUGHEY,
Amsterdam, Jefferson Co., Ohio.

The following letter was written to the Hon. William H. Seward in behalf of the Union men in prison and within the rebel lines.

CENTRAL MILITARY PRISON, Tupelo,
Ittawamba Co., Mississippi, July 11th, 1862.

Hon. William H. Seward:

DEAR SIR—A large number of citizens of Mississippi, holding Union sentiments, and who recognise no such military usurpation as the so-called Confederate States of America, are confined in a filthy prison, swarming with vermin, and are famishing from hunger—a sufficient quantity of food not being furnished us. We are separated from our families, and suffered to hold no communication with them.

We are compelled, under a strong guard, to perform the most menial services, and are insulted on every occasion by the officers and guards of the prison. The nights are very cool; we are furnished with no bedding, and are compelled to lie down on the floor of our dungeon, where sleep seldom visits us, until exhausted nature can hold out no longer; then our slumbers are broken, restless, and of short duration. Our property is confiscated, and our families left destitute of the necessaries of life; all that they have, yea, all their living, being seized upon by the Confederates, and converted to their own use. Heavy fetters are placed upon our limbs, and daily some of us are led to the scaffold, or to death by shooting. Many of us are forced into the army, instant death being the penalty in case of refusal; thus constraining us to bear arms against our country, to become the executioners of our friends and brethren, or to fall ourselves by their hands.

These evils are intolerable, and we ask protection, through you, from the United States Government. The Federal Government may not be able to release us, but we ask the protection which the Federal prisoner receives. Were his life taken, swift retribution would be visited upon the rebels by a just retaliation—a rebel prisoner would suffer death for every Federal prisoner whom they destroyed. Let this rule hold good in the case of Union men who are citizens of the South. The loyal Mississippian deserves protection as much as the loyal native of Massachusetts. We ask, also, that our confiscated property be restored to us, or, in case of our death, to our families. If it be destroyed, let reparation be demanded from the rebels, or the property of known and avowed secessionists sequestered to that use.

Before this letter reaches its destination, the majority of us will have ceased to be. The writer has been informed by the officers that "his chances for living long are very slender;" that he has confessed enough to cause him to lose his life, and the Judge Advocate has specified Tuesday, the 15th inst., as the day of his execution. We have, therefore, little hope that we, individually, can receive any benefit from this petition, though you regard it favourably, and consent to its suggestions; but our families, who have been so cruelly robbed of all their substance, may, in after time, receive remuneration for their great losses. And if citizens of avowed secession proclivities, who are within the Federal lines, are arrested and held as hostages for the safety of Union men who are and may be hereafter incarcerated in the prison in Tupelo and elsewhere, the rebels will not dare put another Union man to death.

Hoping that you will deem it proper to take the matters presented in our petition under advisement, we remain, with high considerations of respect and esteem, your oppressed and imprisoned fellow-citizens,

JOHN H. AUGHEY,
BENJAMIN CLARKE,
JOHN ROBINSON,
and thirty-seven others.

Two young men informed me to-day that they had been forced into the rebel service. They had been taken prisoners at Corinth by General Pope, and had taken the oath of allegiance to the Federal Government, to which their hearts had always been loyal. Recently they had been arrested, and on refusing to rejoin their regiment, were immured in this dungeon. From the threats of the officers, they expected to be shot at any moment. They had used every means to banish the thoughts of death—had forced themselves to engage in pleasantry and mirth to drive away the sadness and gloom which oppressed them when alone, and recalled the pleasures of their happy homes—homes which they would never see again. I counselled them to prepare to meet their God in peace; to wisely improve the short time granted them to make their calling and election sure. They replied that they hoped all would be well. They had long since confessed Christ before men, and hoped for salvation through his merits. Still, they could not help feeling sad in the near prospect of death. They left me to mingle with a group of prisoners, who were endeavouring to dissipate the tedium, and vary the monotonous routine of prison life, by "telling stories." Captain Bruce led off by telling the following Irish story:

"Once upon a time, an Irishman, who rejoiced in the possession of a fine mare and a colt, wished to cross the Mississippi river at Baton Rouge with them. By some mishap, they were all precipitated from the ferry-boat into the water. The Irishman, being unable to swim, grasped the colt's tail, hoping thus to be carried to the shore. Some of the passengers called out to him: 'Halloo, Pat, why don't you take hold of the mare's tail; she is much stronger, and much more able to carry you safely to the shore.' 'O, be jabers!' says Pat, 'this is no time for swapping horses.'" This tale was received with applause.

Baltimore Bill, a real Plug-ugly, told his story next, as follows: "Two Irishmen, immediately after their arrival in America, found a gun. After long inspection, they concluded it was some kind of musical instrument, and wishing to hear the music, it was agreed that Jimmie should blow at the muzzle, while Pat worked with the 'fixins' at the breech. At it they went. Soon the gun went off, and Jimmie fell down, shot dead. 'Och!' says Pat, 'are you charmed at the first note?'" This story was received with loud bursts of laughter. An officer then entered, and ordered us to be quiet, forbidding us to narrate any more tales.

## CHAPTER V.

### EXECUTION OF UNION PRISONERS.

**Resolved to Escape—Mode of Executing Prisoners—Removal of Chain—Addition to our Numbers—Two Prisoners become Insane—Plan of Escape—Proves a Failure—Fetters Inspected—Additional Fetters—Handcuffs—A Spy in the Disguise of a Prisoner—Special Police Guard on Duty—A Prisoner's Discovery—Divine Services—The General Judgment—The Judge—The Laws—The Witnesses—The Concourse—The Sentence.**

On Friday morning, the twelfth of July, as I lay restless and sore, endeavouring to find some position which would be sufficiently easy to permit me to enjoy, even for a few moments, the benefit of "Tired nature's sweet restorer, balmy sleep," the thought occurred that it would be well to attempt an escape, though it should result in death from the fire of the guards, which would be far preferable to death by strangling at the rope's end, and in the presence of a large concourse of rebel enemies. Their method of shooting was, to dig a hole, and make the victim sit with his legs hanging in it. The soldiers would fire three balls through the brain, and three through the heart; then the mangled and bleeding body fell into the grave, and was immediately covered with earth. At first, coffins were used, but of late, these had been dispensed with, owing to the increased expense, and the increasing number of executions.

I had not long meditated upon this subject, when I arose, fully resolved on death or liberty. My intentions were communicated to several prisoners, who promised me all the aid in their power. My fetters were examined, and it was concluded, that with proper instruments my bands could be divested of the iron which secured the chain-rings. A long-handled iron spoon, a knife, and an old file, were obtained, and two were detached at a time to work on my fetters. We went to one side of the building, and a sufficient number of prisoners stood in front of us, to prevent the guard from noticing our proceedings. Our locations were changed frequently, to prevent detection; and when an officer entered, labour was suspended till his exit.

We called General Bragg, Robespierre; General Jordan, Marat; and General Hardee, Danton. Several prisoners were led out and shot to-day. The majority of them were Union men. Six Union men were committed to jail to-day. The horrors of our situation were sufficient to render two of these victims insane. A reign of terror had been inaugurated, only equalled, in its appalling enormity, by the memorable French Revolution. Spies and informers, in the pay of the Rebel government, prowl through the country, using every artifice and strategy to lead Union men to criminate themselves, after which they are dragged to prison and to death. The cavalry dash through the country, burning cotton, carrying off the property of loyal citizens, and committing depredations of every kind.

Several prisoners resolved to attempt an escape with me. Our plan was, to bring in the axe with which we split wood for cooking, and raise a plank in the floor, a sufficient number to stand around those who lifted it, to prevent observation, and then make our way out among the guards, who were off duty on the north side of the building. At this time there were three guards in front of each door, and two on the south side of the building. On the north side of the building, there were no guards on duty, for, if the other three sides were securely guarded, the prisoners could not escape on the north side. There were, however, several hundred guards, who, when off duty, slept on this side of the prison. When their turn came, they went on duty; and those who were relieved, came there to sleep. They were coming and going all the time, and during the whole night, they kept up an incessant noise.

After the unremitting labour of my friends during the day, I found that I could slip my chain off and on at pleasure. The sun was now setting, but the axe had not been brought in. At this time a guard was stationed in each door; the favourable moment had passed; none dared to bring the axe past the guard. While deliberating on the best course to pursue—as raising a plank had proved a failure for the present—General Jordan and Colonel Clare entered. I was standing with others in the middle of the floor. General Jordan came directly to me; either accidentally or intentionally, he held up a light to my face. "Ah! you are here yet," said he. I gave an affirmative nod. "Well," said he to Colonel Clare, "I must examine this fellow's irons." Putting his hand down, and ascertaining that they had been tampered with, he endeavoured, ineffectually, to pull the bands off; he did not notice that I could slip the chain-rings off. "These irons," said he, "are very insecure; who helped you to put them in this condition?" I made no reply. After waiting until he found I intended none, he continued: "Colonel Clare, have these irons secured in the morning; also put handcuffs on him, and chain him, so as to confine him to one locality; the gallows shall not be cheated of their due." Having given these orders, they passed out. As soon as they were gone, the prisoners who had aided me crowded around, stating that they believed there was a spy in the house, in the guise of a prisoner, and declaring that I must escape that night, or it would be too late. All realized that on to-morrow there would be no hope.

There were eleven guards on duty—three in front of each door, one in each door, two on the south side of the building, and at night one passing back and forth through the centre of the prison, which was lighted during the whole night. There was also a special police guard on duty that night, as five Federal prisoners, who remained in our prison until some formalities were gone through with, would be sent in the morning to the prison at Columbus, Mississippi, and it was feared they might attempt to escape ere they were sent further south.

At this juncture, a young man ran up and informed me that he had made a discovery which might result in my escape; I must go alone, however, and though they would aid me, they would run great risk in doing so.

Only four could assist, and he would volunteer to be one of them. Several others immediately volunteered, of whom three were selected by M——, and the plan then communicated. At this moment, Captain Bruce announced that the hour for divine worship had arrived. I asked my friends whether I should plead indisposition, and dispense with the services for that time. They replied that it might lead to suspicion, and advised me to give them a short sermon. I went to my usual place of standing, clanking my chains as heretofore. I give a synopsis of the sermon.

The text was 2 Cor. v. 10: "We must all appear before the judgment-seat of Christ, that every one may receive the things done in his body, according to that he hath done, whether it be good or bad."

The doctrine of a general judgment was revealed to mankind at a very early period of the world's history. Enoch, the seventh from Adam, prophesied, saying, "Behold the Lord cometh with ten thousand of his saints, to execute judgment upon all, and to convince all that are ungodly among them of all their ungodly deeds which they have ungodly committed, and of all their hard speeches which ungodly sinners have spoken against him." Job declares: "I know that my Redeemer liveth, and that he shall stand at the latter day upon the earth." Daniel also speaks of a general judgment: "I beheld till the thrones were cast down, and the Ancient of days did sit, whose garment was white as snow, and the hair of his head like the pure wool: his throne was like the fiery flame, and his wheels as burning fire. A fiery stream issued and came forth from before him: thousand thousands ministered unto him, and ten thousand times ten thousand stood before him: the judgment was set, and the books were opened." The New Testament is also explicit in its declarations that God hath appointed a day in which he will judge the world in righteousness by that man whom he hath ordained. The text declares that we must all appear before the judgment-seat of Christ.

The scenes which will usher in the judgment

of the great day will be of the most magnificent character. "The heavens shall pass away with a great noise, and the elements shall melt with fervent heat; the earth also, and the works that are therein, shall be burned up." This does not indicate annihilation. God will never annihilate any of his creatures, animate or inanimate.

The inquiry is often made, what becomes of the soul after death, and where does it await the general judgment? A sect called the Soul-sleepers, take the position that the soul, after death, goes into a torpid state, like bears in winter, and thus remains till the sounding of the Archangel's trump. There is no Scripture to sustain this view, and it is only assumed, to avoid the objection that God would not judge a soul, and send it to reward or punishment, and then bring it back, to be again judged. That the soul, at death, passes immediately into glory or torment, is proved by many scriptures. Paul "desired to depart, and be with Christ, which was far better," than remaining on earth. He declares that to be present with the body, is to be absent from the Lord. The dying Stephen calls upon the Lord Jesus to receive his spirit. These holy men would not thus have spoken, if they supposed that ages must elapse ere they entered heaven. God is not the God of the dead or torpid, but of the living. Moses and Elias appeared on the mount of transfiguration in a state far from torpidity. The dying thief received the promise, "This day shalt thou be with me in paradise." No mention is made of Purgatory or torpidity. The objector urges that paradise is not heaven. We are told that the river of life flows from the throne of God, that the tree of life grows on both sides of the river, and that the tree of life grows in the midst of the paradise of God. The paradise of God is where he is seated on his throne, which is heaven. Paradise is where Christ is. The thief would be with Christ in paradise. He who regards the Lord Jesus as the Chief among ten thousand, the One altogether lovely, will deem his presence heaven indeed. As to the wicked, it is said of the rich man, that in hell he lifted up his eyes, being in torment. If, after being judged, the souls of believers, do pass immediately into glory, and the wicked into torment, what use is there of another or general judgment. I reply, We are responsible not only for our acts, but for the influence which those acts exert through all time. Gibbon, Hume, Rosseau, Paine, and other infidel writers, wrote works which, during the life of the authors, did great evil. If those wicked men passed away from earth impenitent, they are now suffering the vengeance of eternal fire. But the influence for evil, of those wicked works, did not cease with the death of their authors. Thousands of young men every year are led into pernicious and hurtful errors by their perusal. At the general judgment, the accumulated guilt, for the baleful influence exerted through their writings in all time, will sink them deeper in the flames of perdition. The sainted Alexander, and other pious men who are now in heaven, wrote many works whose influence for good was great while their authors lived; and since their death they are, and will continue to be, instrumental in the hand of God in turning many to righteousness. All the good accomplished by their writings, through all time, will, at the judgment, add to their exceeding and eternal weight of glory.

In this life, we often see the righteous man contending with life's unnumbered woes; all the dealings of Providence seem to be adverse. While the wicked are in great power, they flourish in life, like the green bay-tree, and have no bands in their death. These things are strange and mysterious. We understand them not now; but we shall learn, in that great day, when all mysteries are made plain, that God's dealings were just, both with the righteous and the wicked.

The text declares that *we* must all appear before the judgment-seat of Christ. This *we* includes all who are now within the sound of my voice, and not only us, but all who live upon the face of the earth; and the Archangel's trump will wake the pale nations of the dead, and summon them to judgment. The dark domain of hell will be vacated, and the angels that kept not their first estate, and are now reserved in chains of darkness, will appear in the presence of the Judge. Heaven's holy inhabitants will be present. Thus heaven, earth, and hell, will be represented in that august assemblage. The scene will bear some resemblance to that which takes place in our earthly courts. The Lord Jesus Christ will be the Judge, and the angels and saints will be the jurors, who will consent to and approve of the acts of the Judge. The angels will be the officers who will summon, from the prison-house of hell, the devils, to the trial, and also those wicked men who will call upon the rocks and mountains to fall upon them, and hide them from the face of the Lamb. Nor, as is so often the case with earthly officers, will any be able to elude the vigilance of these. They will be clothed with ample power to compel the attendance of all; none will escape. We *must all* appear before the judgment-seat. As in earthly courts, law is the basis of judgment, so we shall be judged according to law in that day. The heathen will be judged by the law of nature—the law written in their hearts, and on their consciences. The light of nature teaches the being, wisdom, power, and goodness of God. For a violation of this law, they will be beaten with few stripes. The Jews will be judged by both the law of nature, which they have, in common with the heathen and the Mosaic law. But we who live in the nineteenth century, in the full blaze of gospel light, will be judged not only by the light of nature and the Mosaic law, which we possess in common with the heathen and the Jew, but also by the glorious gospel of the Son of God, which brought life and immortality to light; and if condemned, how fearful our doom, who are so highly favoured! In earthly courts, we are judged for our overt acts alone; but in the court of heaven, the commandment is exceeding broad; it reaches every thought. Our words, too, are taken into account. We must give an account for every idle word. By our words, we shall be justified, and by our words we shall be condemned. Our thoughts, our words, our deeds, will all be taken into account.

As in our courts there are witnesses, so also there will be at the bar of God. Our pious relatives and friends will bear this testimony, that they have prayed with us and for us; that they had a deep concern for our souls, and that we who are found on the left hand of the Judge, refused all their counsel, and despised their admonitions. Ministers of the gospel will testify that they came as ambassadors from the King of kings, and beseeching you, in Christ's stead, to be reconciled to God, pointing to the coming wrath, and warning you from that wrath to flee; and yet their labour of love ye despised, and scorned the message from on high. The Bible will be a witness against you. Its teachings are able to make wise unto salvation. It is the chart which is given to guide us through this wilderness-world, to fairer worlds on high. It tells of the Lamb of God, who taketh away the sin of the world. It is truth without any mixture of error, and yet you have despised this necessary revelation, and chosen to perish, with the Word of Life open before you. God, the

Father, will be a swift witness against you. In the greatness of his love for you, in the counsels of eternity, he devised the plan of salvation, and sent his only begotten Son to suffer and die, that you might live, and yet you have despised that love, and rejected that Saviour. God, the Son, will bear this testimony, that he came from the shining abodes of glory, where seraphim and cherubim fell prostrate at his feet, in humble adoration, and emptying himself of his glory, bore all the ills of life—the persecutions of wicked men, and the accursed death of the cross, that salvation might be yours, and yet ye refused it, and trod the blood of the Son of God under foot, and put him to an open shame. The Holy Spirit, the Third Person of the adorable Trinity, will bear witness that he often knocked at the door of your hearts for admittance; that he wooed you to embrace his love, offering to abide with you for ever, and yet you rejected the offer, and did despite to the Spirit of grace, till, in sorrow, he took his everlasting flight.

The devil is now going about as a roaring

lion, seeking whom he may devour, and sometimes transforming himself into an angel of light. He is tempting you to sin, by presenting before your minds the superior charms of the riches and pleasures of earth, to things that are unseen and eternal. He has no power to compel you to sin. His evil suggestions are whispered in your oft too willing ears, and then it remains with you to accept or reject. He has no power of compulsion. Your sin must be an act of your own will, or it is not sin. When you consent to the wiles of this arch enemy, and sin against God, remember that with eager desire and base ingratitude he will fiercely accuse in the great day of God Almighty, and urge these very sins of his suggestion as a reason why he should have you to torment you for ever in the bottomless pit.

That internal monitor, that light which enlightens every man that cometh into the world—the moral sense, or conscience—will be a swift witness against you. By it you have been enlightened and warned; and in the case of many who have denied a future state of punishment, the goadings of remorse have convinced them that there is a hell, the kindlings of whose fires they have felt in their own bosoms. Conscience will compel you to confess that your doom is just, though for ever debarred from the joys and happiness of heaven. O! my fellow-prisoners and travellers to the bar of God, listen to her warning voice to-day, before it be too late, and you are compelled mournfully to exclaim, "The harvest is past, the summer is ended, and I am not saved!" The conscience of the sinner will be compelled to admit the truth of the testimony. In earthly courts, oftentimes witnesses are suborned, and their testimony false. Not so at the grand assize. Not a scrap of false testimony will be admitted. The evidence will be in truth, and the judgment in righteousness.

After all these scenes have occurred, the Judge will render a verdict, and pronounce the sentence, which will be irreversible and eternal. With regard to the righteous, though they have been guilty of many sins, both of omission and commission, and have no merits of their own to plead, and consider themselves justly obnoxious to eternal banishment, their Advocate, the Lord Jesus Christ, in whom, while in the flesh, they exercised a true and living faith, will now present them, clad in the white robes of his perfect righteousness, faultless before his Father, and they will now hear the welcome plaudit, "Come ye blessed, inherit the kingdom prepared for you from the foundation of the world." But those on the left hand, who all their life rejected the mercy offered—the great salvation proffered without money and without price—will now hear the dread sentence, "Depart, ye cursed, into everlasting fire, prepared for the devil and his angels!"

O my dear, impenitent fellow-prisoners! how can ye take up your abode, your eternal abode, in everlasting burnings? How can ye dwell with devouring fire? How can ye endure everlasting destruction from the presence of the Lord and the glory of his power, shut up for ever in the fearful pit out of which there is no egress except for the vision of the damned, and the smoke of its torment? Be wise to-day, 'tis madness to defer. Procrastination is the thief of time. Delay is fraught with awful danger. Trust not in promises of future amendment. The way to hell is paved with good resolutions, which are never kept. The future convenient season never arrives. Like Felix, we may tremble when the minister reasons of a judgment to come; and like Agrippa, we may be almost persuaded to be a Christian, and yet come short of the glory of God through procrastination. Procrastination has populated hell. All the doomed and damned from Christian lands are victims of this pernicious and destructive wile of the devil. It is foolish to procrastinate. Though the Bible teems with rich and glorious promises of a hundred-fold blessings in this life, and eternal glory in the world to come, to those who break off their sins by righteousness, and their transgressions by turning unto the Lord, yet all these promises are limited to the present tense. There is not a single blessing promised the future penitent. He procrastinates at the risk of losing all. Behold, *now* is the accepted time, and *now* is the day of salvation. *To-day* if ye will hear his voice, harden not your hearts. "Ho, every one that thirsteth, *come* ye to the waters; and he that hath no money, *come* ye, *buy* and *eat;* yea, *come buy* wine and milk without money and without price." "Seek ye *first* the kingdom of God and his righteousness." "And the Spirit and the Bride say, *come;* let him that heareth say, *come;* and let him that is athirst *come:* and whosoever will, let him *take* the water of life freely."

Choose ye *this day* whom ye will serve. There is no warrant for deferring till to-morrow the momentous and eternal interests of the immortal soul. The shortness and uncertainty of life furnish a strong reason why we should not procrastinate. In the Bible, life is compared to everything that is swift, transient, and fleeting in its nature. It is compared to the swoop of the eagle hasting to the prey; to the swift post, to the bubble on the river. Life is compared in its duration to a year, a day, and to nothing, yea, less than nothing, and vanity.

All these comparisons indicate that it is very brief and evanescent. We have no lease of life; we hold it by a very slight tenure; and this is especially true of us in our present condition. Confined in prison, some of us led to death every day without a moment's warning, every evening I address some who, before the next evening, are in eternity. Myself in chains, my life declared forfeited, ought we not all to be deeply impressed with the necessity of immediate preparation to meet our God? I feel that I am preaching as a dying man to dying men, and I beseech you in Christ's stead, be ye reconciled to God. Believe in the Lord Jesus Christ, and ye shall be saved. Trust in him for salvation, for he is faithful who has promised. God has never said to any, seek ye my face in vain. By the love and mercy of God, by the terrors of the judgment, by the sympathy and compassion of Jesus, I entreat you, my fellow-prisoners, to seek an interest, a present interest, in the great salvation!

I close for the present. We shall never all engage in divine service together again on earth. We separate—some to go to a distant prison, and some to death. May God grant that when we are done with earthly scenes, we may all meet in the realms of bliss, where there is in God's presence fulness of joy, and at his right hand pleasures for evermore! And may the love of God, the grace of our Lord Jesus Christ, and the communion of the Holy Spirit, rest and abide with us, and all the Israel of God, now, henceforth, and for ever, Amen!

The following hymn was then sung:

In the sun, and moon, and stars,
Signs and wonders there shall be;
Earth shall quake with inward wars,
Nations with perplexity.

Soon shall ocean's hoary deep,
Tossed with stronger tempests, rise;
Wilder storms the mountains sweep,
Louder thunders rock the skies.

Dread alarms shall shake the proud,
Pale amazement, restless fear;
And, amid the thunder-cloud,
Shall the Judge of men appear.

> But though from his awful face,
> Heaven shall fade, and earth shall fly,
> Fear not ye, his chosen race,
> Your redemption draweth nigh.

I preached longer than I had intended, having become so fully engrossed with the subject as to forget my chains and my frustrated plans. My fellow-prisoners were listening apparently with interest; great solemnity prevailed, and penitential tears were flowing. It was evident that the Spirit of the living God was in our midst; and though danger and death were before our eyes, the consolations of the glorious gospel of the blessed God caused our peace to flow like a river. The precious seed was sown in tears. May we not entertain a good hope that he who cast the seed into this soil, prepared by affliction, shall come again with rejoicing, bringing his sheaves with him. By my side stood two in chains, who appeared deeply moved. During the day I had conversed with them about their souls. They expressed regret that they had not heretofore given this matter the attention its importance demanded. Since their imprisonment, however, they had been led to feel that they were great sinners, and had, as they hoped, put their trust in Christ alone for salvation. I have since learned that on the morrow they were shot.

## CHAPTER VI.

### SUCCESSFUL ESCAPE.

The Second Plan of Escape—Under the Jail—Egress—Among the Guards—In the Swamp—Travelling on the Underground Railroad—The Fare—Green Corn eaten Raw—Blackberries and Stagnant Water—The Blood-hounds—Tantalizing Dreams—The Pickets—The Cows—Become Sick—Fons Beatus—Find Friends—Union Friend No. Two—The night in the Barn—Death of Newman by Scalding—Union Friend No. Three—Bound for the Union Lines—Rebel Soldiers—Black Ox—Pied Ox—Reach Headquarters in Safety—Emotions on again beholding the Old Flag—Kindness while Sick—Meeting with his Family—Richard Malone again—The Serenade—Leave Dixie—Northward bound.

After the sermon was concluded, the preparations for my escape were commenced. The building used for our prison was built with the front toward the east. The doors were at the eastern and western extremities, which were the gable ends, one door being in each end. There were also two windows at each end, the door being between them. The doors and window-sashes had been removed, to allow the guards stationed in front an unobstructed view of the interior. At night the apartment was lighted, and a guard patrolled the floor; it was, therefore, nearly impossible for a person to escape the observation of the guards, either within or without the jail. In the North, the houses are usually built with a cellar underneath; at the South, such a thing is very rare, the houses being built upon the ground, or upon piles. Our prison was built upon piles, the floor being elevated about eighteen inches above the ground. The boards were nailed upon the building perpendicularly, and in some cases did not quite reach to the ground. Small openings were thus left between the floor and the ground, through which a person could crawl underneath the building. Around each door was an enclosure, formed by stakes surmounted with poles, in the shape of a parallelogram, whose dimensions were about ten by sixteen feet. In each of these enclosures four guards were stationed, one of them being seated in the doorway. The rear enclosure was used for cooking purposes; and into both enclosures we were permitted to go at pleasure during all hours of the day, and as late at night as ten o'clock. Only three prisoners were allowed to be in an enclosure at one time.

M—— had discovered a hole by the side of the steps within the front enclosure, by which I could get under the building. I felt unwilling to make such an attempt, as the aperture was in the immediate vicinity of the guards. M—— stated that four others would aid me, though at considerable risk on their part. "I'll take the risk," was the individual response of all present. M—— selected three, who with himself assumed the perilous task, in which discovery would have cost them their lives. M——, who had devised the plan of escape, now instructed us in the respective parts we were to perform. All promised implicit obedience. At half-past nine, three prisoners and myself were to go into the enclosure. They would stand up and converse with the guards, whilst I sat upon the ground by the hole, to wait for an opportunity to crawl under the building unobserved. This opportunity we expected to occur at ten o'clock, when the relief-guard came on duty. The duty of one prisoner was to remain inside and engage the attention of the guard who sat in the doorway, while the other three would go into the enclosure, and entertain the other guards, according to the previously devised plan. At half-past nine o'clock, we placed ourselves in the designated positions. I readily removed my chain, coiled it up, and laid it by the side of a little stump. The moon shone with great brilliancy, revealing the tents which surrounded us on every side. Officers and soldiers passed hurriedly to and fro. We were in the midst of the noise and confusion of a great encampment, as there were in and around Tupelo some fifteen thousand soldiers. Mingled sounds of mirth and contention proceeded from the surrounding tents. My prisoner friends were engaged in a fierce argument with the guards as to the comparative merits of Tennessee and Mississippi troops. This was done to divert their attention, and I observed with pleasure that they were meeting with success. I reflected that a few more moments would decide my fate. If detected, my life must end ignominiously and on the gallows. In the morning, my anklets would be securely welded. I would also be handcuffed and chained to a post. Then all hope must end, and soon my corpse would be borne into the presence of her whose tears were flowing, and who refused to be comforted because of my ominous absence.

The order for the relief-guard now came loud and clear. I heard their hurried tramp, and saw their glittering bayonets in the bright moonlight. The set time, the appointed moment, big with my fate, had arrived. I offered an ejaculatory prayer to Him who sits upon the throne of heaven for protection at this critical moment. The guard stood within ten feet of me, with their eyes constantly upon me. Just as they were turning to receive the advancing relief-guard, I crawled backward under the building, and disappeared from their view. The relief-guard went on duty, and those relieved retired. The prisoners were ordered into the house, and as the new guards

"Just as they were turning to receive the relief-guard, I crawled backward under the building, and disappeared from view." Page 172.

did not know that four were in the enclosure, I was not missed.

I was now under the prison, but there were guards on every side, and the jail was in the midst of a camp, so that I was still in great danger of detection. I saw, through the crevices in the floor, the guard who patrolled the prison. I heard the murmurings and mutterings of the prisoners, as he occasionally trod upon them in his carelessness. I could hear, though not distinctly, the conversation of the prisoners. One of my assistants was detailing to his companions their success in getting me off unnoticed. The prisoners slept but little that night, owing to their anxiety for my safety, and I frequently heard my name mentioned, and hopes for my safety expressed. I occasionally fell into uneasy slumbers, but the fleas and other vermin were so annoying, that my sleep refreshed me but little. I could distinctly hear the new guard conversing, and among other topics, one remarked that he had forgotten the countersign; the other replied that it was *Braxton*. Well, said the former, I thought it was Bragg, or Braxton, or something like that. Knowing the countersign emboldened me, as I could, if halted, give it, and pass on. I soon crawled to the north side of the prison, and found that there were three apertures sufficiently large to admit of my egress. Upon reaching the first one, I found a number of guards, some sitting and some lying so close to it, that I dared not make the attempt at that point.

Crawling to the second, I remained till there was comparative quiet; but at the instant I was about to pass out, a soldier, who was lying with his face toward me, commenced to cough, and continued to do so, at intervals, for more than an hour. Finding it unadvisable to run the risk of detection at this point, I made my way, with considerable difficulty, to the third and last aperture, near the rear of the building, and not very distant from the rear-guards. I remained at this aperture till I heard one guard say to another that it was three o'clock, and that they must soon go on duty. I felt confident that then was my time, or never, as morning would find me under the house, and

I would be re-arrested in that situation. Committing myself into the hands of God, and asking him to keep me from detection, and grant me a safe escape, I arose from under the building, passed by two sleeping guards, who were lying within three or four feet of the prison. As it was my first essay at walking without chains, I reeled, as if under the influence of strong drink, striking my foot against the head of one of those sleeping guards, who, awaking, turned over, and uttering some exclamation of disapprobation, took no further notice of me, doubtless mistaking me for one of his companions. After proceeding a few steps, I sat down upon the ground among some of the guards. I took out my knife, and whistling, to appear as unconcerned as possible, commenced whittling a stump, around which they were collected—some sitting, some standing, and others reclining. I readily passed for one of them, as I was wearing a colored shirt, which resembled that worn by the guards. I soon, however, arose, and wound my way among the various groups, endeavouring to reach the corn-field, to which I had made my first escape. After passing the guards off duty, a sentinel arose a short distance in front of me, evidently with the intention of halting me, if I advanced farther. Stopping a few minutes, to avoid suspicion, I changed my direction, bearing southwest, and after a time, got into the woods. Kneeling down, I returned God thanks for thus crowning my efforts with success, and prayed for his continuous protection, and that he would choose out my path, that I might escape detection, and rejoin my family and friends in safety.

I now pursued my journey rapidly in a southwest direction, choosing that which led directly from my home, for two reasons. The cavalry and bloodhounds would not be so likely to follow in that direction, and after listening, while in prison, to the drum-beat morning and evening, in the various surrounding camps, I noticed that it had ceased in the southwest for several mornings; hence I supposed that the camp in that direction had been broken up, and that, in taking that route,

I could more readily get beyond the rebel pickets, and then I could change my course, and bear northward, and reach the Federal lines at some point on the Memphis and Charleston railroad. I hastened on till the sun arose, having passed through woods and cornfields, studiously avoiding all roads, when, as I was rapidly travelling along a narrow path, I met a negro. The suddenness of our meeting alarmed both. I, in a peremptory tone, addressed him, in quick succession, the following interrogatories:

"Where are you going? To whom do you belong? Where have you been? Have you a pass?"

"I belong," said the boy, trembling, "to Mr. ——. I have been to wife's house; am gwine back home, but I haint got nary pass."

"I suppose it is all right with you?"

"Oh, yes, master! it's all right wid me."

Concluding that it was not all right "wid" myself, I hurried on, soon leaving the path, and turning into a dense woods. Travelling on till about one P. M., I came to an open country, so extensive that I could not go round it, neither could I, in daylight, travel through it with safety. I sought out a place to hide, and finding a ditch which bisected a corn-field, I concealed myself in that. During the day, negroes and whites passed near, without discovering me. Becoming hungry, I ate a small piece of the bread which one of my fellow-prisoners had given me, but it made me quite sick. On my former escape, I had, just before leaving the house, traded pants with a fellow-prisoner, without his knowledge or consent. On my return, he refused to trade back. My reason for trading was, to get a dark pair, as mine were so light-coloured, I feared the guards would discover me more readily. Their owner had been accustomed to use tobacco, and the bread had become tinctured with it. Tobacco being very offensive to me, its presence on my bread caused me to lose it.

The day passed away, and the night came. The stars came out in silent glory, one by one. Fixing my eye upon the pole-star, the underground railroad travellers' guide, I set out, bearing a little to the west of north. I soon reached the thick woods, and found it very difficult to make rapid progress, in consequence of the dense under-growth and obscure light. The bushes would strike me in the eyes, and often the top of a fallen tree would cause me to make quite a circuit. Soon, however, the moon arose in her brightness—the old silver moon. But her light I found to be far less brilliant than that of the sun, and her rays were much obscured by the dense foliage overhead; hence my progress was necessarily slow, laboured, and toilsome. I slept but little during the day, in consequence of the proximity of those who might be bitter foes, and also the unpleasant position I occupied, as the ditch in which I had concealed myself was muddy, and proved an uncomfortable bed. I therefore became weary, my limbs stiff from travel and from the pressure of the heavy iron bands. Sleep overpowered me, and I laid down in the leaves, and slept till the cold awoke me, which, judging from the moon's descent, must have been an hour and a half. The nights in Mississippi are invariably cool, however hot the days may be. Arising from my uneasy slumber, I pressed on. My thirst, which for some time had been increasing, now became absolutely unendurable. I knew not where to obtain water, not daring to go near a well, through fear of being arrested. At length I heard some suckling pigs and their dam, at a short distance from me, in the woods. There seemed to be no alternative. I must either perish, or obtain some fluid to slake my raging thirst; so I resolved to catch a little pig, cut its throat, and drink the blood. I searched for my knife, but I had lost it. I was, therefore, reluctantly compelled to abandon my design on the suckling's life. As I went forward, the sow and her brood started up alarmed, and in their flight, plunged into water. I immediately followed, and found a mud-hole. Removing the green scum, I drank deep of the stagnant pool. My thirst was only partially quenched by this draught, and soon returned. As day dawned, I found some sassafras leaves, which

I chewed, to allay the pangs of hunger; but they formed a paste which I could not swallow.

I soon after came to an old field, where I obtained an abundant supply of blackberries, which not only served to check the gnawings of hunger, but also to allay my intolerable thirst. I reflected that this day was the holy Sabbath, but it brought neither rest to my weary frame, nor composure to my agitated and excited mind. Like Salathiel, the Wandering Jew, the word *March!* was ringing in my ears. Onward! was my motto; Liberty or death! my watchword. About ten o'clock I came to an open country, and sought out a ditch, in which to conceal myself. Here I fell into a troubled sleep. I saw, in dreams, tables groaning under the weight of the most delicious viands, and brooks of crystal waters, bubbling and sparkling as they rushed onward in their meandering course; but when I attempted to grasp them, they served me as they did Tantalus, of olden time, by vanishing into thin air, or receding beyond my reach. While lying here, I was now and then aroused by the trampling of horses grazing in the field, which I feared might be bringing on my pursuers. And once the voices of men, mingled with the sounds of horses' feet upon a little bridge, some twenty feet distant, induced me to look out from my hiding-place, and lo! two cavalry-men—perhaps hunting for my life!—rode along.

When the sun had reached the zenith, I was again startled by voices, which approached nearer and nearer my place of concealment, till at length the cause was discovered. Several children, both black and white, had come from a farm-house, about a quarter of a mile distant, to gather blackberries along the margin of the ditch. They soon discovered me, and seemed somewhat startled and alarmed at my appearance. I soon saw them gazing down upon me, in my moist bed, with evident amazement and alarm. Pallid, haggard, unshaven, and covered with mud, I must have presented a frightful picture.

As soon as the children passed me, fearing the report they would carry home, I arose from my lair, and hurried on, though I had to pass in sight of several houses. After travelling three or four miles through an open champaign country, I came to a dense woods, bordering a stream which had ceased running, in consequence of the great drought that had, for a long time, prevailed throughout this section of Mississippi. The creek had been a large one, and in the deep holes, some water still remained, though warm, and covered with a heavy scum, and mingled with the spawn of frogs. I drank it, however, from sheer necessity, tepid and unhealthy as it was. It did not allay my thirst, but created a nausea, which was very unpleasant.

About four o'clock P. M., I was startled by the baying of bloodhounds behind me, and apparently on my track. Before escaping from jail, I had been advised by the prisoners to obtain some onions, as these, rubbed on the soles of my boots, would destroy the scent. They could only be procured, however, by a visit to some garden-patch, and I feared to go so near a house. I had left no clothes in prison from which the hounds could obtain the scent in order to find my track, and my starting in a southwest direction was an additional precaution against bloodhounds. Their baying soon became alarmingly distinct. Having heard them almost every night for years, as they hunted down the fugitive slave, I could not mistake the fearful import of their howling. I could devise no plan for breaking the trail. Dan Boone, when pursued by Indians, succeeded in baffling the hounds by catching at some overhanging branches, and swinging himself forward. Negroes often destroy the scent by carrying matches, and setting the leaves on fire. One negro of whom I heard, ran along the brink of a precipice, and dug a recess back from the narrow path. Crawling into it, he remained till the hounds reached that point, when he thrust them from the path. They fell and were dashed to pieces on the jagged rocks below.

None of these plans were practicable to me, and I supposed death imminent, either from being torn to pieces by the hounds, or by being shot by the cavalry, who were following them.

Climbing a tree, I resolved to await the arrival of the cavalry, and having determined to die rather than be taken back again to Tupelo, I would refuse to obey any summons to descend. O, how I wished for my navy repeater, that I might sell my life as dearly as possible! that I might make some secessionist bite the dust ere I was slain! I often thought of the couplet in the old song—

> "The hounds are baying on my track,
> Christian, will you send me back?"

A feeling of strong sympathy arose in my bosom for the poor African, who, in his endeavour to escape from the Iron Furnace of Southern slavery, often encountered the blood-hounds, and was torn to pieces by them. "A fellow feeling makes us wondrous kind."

I had remained but a short time in the tree, when I ascertained that the hounds were bearing eastward, and they soon passed at a distance. They were on the track of some other poor fugitive, and I rejoiced again in the hope of safety. Coming to a corn-field, I plucked two ears of corn, and ate them raw, having no matches wherewith to kindle a fire, which, indeed, would have increased my peril, as the smoke might advertise my presence to bitter and unrelenting foes.

Toward night I lay down in the woods, and fell asleep. Visions of abundance, both to eat and drink, haunted me, and every unusual sound would startle me. A fly peculiar to the South, whose buzz sounded like the voice of an old man, often awoke me with the fear that my enemies were near. As soon as Ursa Minor appeared, I took up my line of march. The night was very dark, and I became somewhat bewildered. At length I reached a cross-roads, and as I was emerging from the wood, I saw two pickets a few yards from me. Stooping down, I crawled on my hands and knees back into the woods. As I retired, I heard one picket say to the other, "Who is that?"

He replied, "It is the lieutenant of the guard."

"What does he want?" said the first.

"He is slipping round to see if we are asleep."

After I got a safe distance in the bushes, I lay down and slept till the moon arose. To the surprise of my bewildered brain, it seemed to rise in the west. Taking my course, I hastened on, sometimes through woods, sometimes through cornfields, and sometimes through swamps. Coming to a large pasture, in which a number of cows were grazing, I tried to obtain some milk, but none of them would allow me to approach near enough to effect my purpose. My face was not of the right colour, and my costume belonged to a sex that never milked them. I travelled until day-break, when I concealed myself in a thicket of cane, and had scarcely fallen asleep when I heard the sound of the reveille, in a camp close at hand. Arising, I hurriedly beat a retreat, and travelled several hours before I dared take any rest. I at length lay down amid the branches of a fallen tree, and slept. Visions of home and friends flitted before me. Voices sweet and kind greeted me on all sides. The bitter taunts of cruel officers no longer assailed my ears. The loved ones at home were present, and the joys of the past were renewed. But, alas! the falling of a limb dissipated all my fancied pleasures. The reality returned, and I was still a fugitive escaping for life, and in the midst of a hostile country.

To-day my mock trial would have taken place, and I fancied the disappointment of Woodruff, who had stated that to his knowledge I was a spy, and to-day would have sworn it. And Barnes, the mail-robber, recommended for promotion because of his heroism in re-arresting me, how sad he must feel, that the bird had flown, and that he would not have the pleasure of witnessing my execution. I thanked God and took courage. Though faint and weary, I was still hopeful and trusting, often repeating,

> "'Tis God has led me safe thus far,
> And he will bring me home."

On this (Monday) night, I travelled steadily, crossing swamps, corn-fields, woods, and pastures. I came to only one cotton-field during the night. I passed through several wheat-fields, where the wheat had been harvested; I pulled a handful from a shock, and rubbed out some of the grain, but it was so bitter I could not eat it. I suspected every bush a secessionist, though I felt much more secure at night than in daylight. I avoided roads as much as possible, travelling on none except to cross them, which was done with great rapidity. The rising sun still found me pressing onward, and thirst and hunger were now consuming me. To satisfy hunger, I had recourse to the corn-field; but I could find no water. I would gladly have drank any kind of beverage, however filthy, so that my thirst might be allayed. About nine o'clock, when I had almost despaired of getting water at all, I came to a copious fountain in a gorge of the hills, and from its appearance, I seemed to be the discoverer. Around it there was no trace of human foot, nor hoof of cattle. On beholding it, I wept with joy. I remained by it about four hours, quaffing its cool and crystal waters, the first running water I had tasted since leaving prison. I also bathed my body and washed my clothes, drying them in the sun, and endeavoured to rid them of vermin, in which I only partially succeeded. I named this fountain *Fons Beatus*, and left it with sincere sorrow.

Three o'clock, P. M., arrived, and I felt bewildered. I knew not where I was. I might be near friends, I might be near bloodthirsty foes. I could scarcely walk. My iron bands had become very irksome. I felt that I was becoming childish. I could tell all my bones. I tried to pray, but could only utter, "Lord, be merciful to me, a sinner!" Still I felt thankful that it was so well with me as it was.

At that very hour, had I not escaped, I should have been either on the scaffold at Tupelo, or suspended between heaven and earth, surrounded by an insulting and jeering army. This reflection made me thankful to God, even though I should die in the swamps. The sky became overcast, and I found it impossible to distinguish north from south. I therefore concealed myself and slept. It was night when I awoke, and the clouds still covered the sky threateningly, concealing my guiding star, and rendering it impossible for me to proceed. Thus, when I wished most to go forward, my progress was arrested, and my distressing suspense prolonged. During the whole night I was asleep and awake alternately, but could not at any time discern either moon or stars. Once, while sleeping behind a fallen tree by the roadside, a horseman passed by. His dog, a large and ferocious-looking animal, came running along by the side of the tree where I was lying. When he reached me, I raised up suddenly and brandishing a club menacingly, the alarmed and howling dog incontinently and ingloriously fled, leaving me master of the field.

On Wednesday morning the sun was still obscured until nine o'clock. I was then sick. There was a ringing in my ears, and I was affected with vertigo, a dimness of vision and faintness, which rendered me absolutely unfit for travel. It required an hour to walk a quarter of a mile. I found a good supply of blackberries, which very much refreshed me.

Before me was a hill, the top of which I reached after two hours' laborious ascent. I despaired of getting much further. I thought I must perish in the Iron Furnace of secession, which was heated very hot for me. Feeling confident that I must be near Tippah county, and knowing that there were many Union men in that county, I resolved to call at the first house on my route. If I remained where I was, I must perish, as I could go no further, and if I met with a Union family, I should be saved; if with "a secesh," I might possibly impose upon their credulity, and get refreshment without being arrested. They might, however, cause my arrest. It was a dilemma such as I hope never to be placed in again. About an hour before sunset I came to a house, and remained near it for some time. At length I saw a negro girl come to the door. Knowing that where there were negroes, in nine cases out of ten there were secessionists near, I left the house as quickly as my enfeebled condition would permit. Going to another house, I remained near it till I was satisfied there were no negroes held by that family. I then went boldly up, knocked, gained admittance, and asked for some water, which was given me. The lady of the house, scrutinizing me closely, asked me if I were from Tupelo. I replied in the affirmative. She then inquired my name. I gave her my Christian name, John Hill, suppressing the surname. Her husband was sitting near, a man of Herculean frame; and as the wife's inquisitiveness was beginning to alarm me, I turned to him and said: "My friend, you are a man of great physical powers, and at this time you ought to be in the army. The Yankees are overrunning all our country, and the service of every man is needed." His wife replied that he was not in the army, nor would he go into it, unless he was forced to go. They had been told that the cavalry would be after him in a few days, to take him as a conscript; but she considered the conscript law, base and tyrannical. Overjoyed at the utterance of such sentiments as these, I then revealed my true character. I told them that I had recently made my escape from Tupelo, where I was doomed to execution on

17

the gallows, and that I was now flying from prison and from death. I then exhibited the iron bands upon my ankles. Both promised all the aid in their power. The lady at once proposed to prepare supper, but I was too near the point of starvation to await the slow process of cooking. She therefore turned down the table-cloth, which covered the fragments remaining from dinner, and disclosed some corn bread and Irish potatoes. Though I never liked corn bread, I must confess I thought that was the sweetest morsel I had ever tasted.

After eating a little, however, I became very sick, and was compelled to desist. It was so long since I had partaken of any substantial food, that my stomach now could not bear it. The lady soon prepared supper, consisting of broiled chicken, and other delicacies. The fowl was quite small, and I ate nearly the whole of it, much to the chagrin of a little daughter of mine host, whom I heard complaining to her mother, afterward, in an adjoining room, saying, "Ma, all I got of that chicken was a little piece of the wing," and "aint that gentleman a hoss to eat?" with other remarks by no means complimentary to my voracious appetite.

After supper, mine host endeavoured to remove the heavy iron bands by which my ankles were clasped. This was accomplished after considerable labour. I asked him to retain the bands till called for, which he promised to do. The good lady furnished me with water and a suit of her husband's clothes. After performing a thorough ablution, I donned the suit, and felt completely metamorphosed, and was thoroughly disguised, as my new suit had been made for a man of vastly larger physical proportions. I spent the night with my new friends, during which a heavy thunder-storm passed over. Had I been out in the drenching rain in my wretched condition, I must surely have perished. In the morning my host informed me of a Union man who knew the country in the direction of Rienzi, the point which I now determined to reach. This gentleman lived half a mile distant, and my host accompanied me to a thicket near his house, where I concealed myself till he brought Mr. —— to me. Said my friend No. 2, "I am not familiar with the route to Rienzi, but will go with you to friend No. 3, who I am positive is well acquainted with the road. He can take you through the woods, so as to avoid the Confederate cavalry. As I undertake this at the risk of my life, we must wait till night. I would gladly have you come to my house, but I fear that it might transpire through my children that I had helped you to escape. I have a large family, and most of 'em is gals, and you know gals will talk. You can stay in my barn till I come for you. I will carry you provisions during the day, and to-night we will go to my friend's."

About three o'clock in the morning, he came with two horses, one of which he mounted, and I the other. The horse I rode was a blooded animal, and to use my friend's expression, could run like a streak of lightning. I provided myself with a good whip, resolving, in case of danger, to put my horse to his utmost speed. A short time after daylight, we reached friend

No. 3, who promised to conduct me to Rienzi. While at his house, I learned that a Unionist, Mr. N——, had been killed under circumstances of the greatest cruelty. His sentiments had become known to the rebels. He was arrested by their cavalry, and refusing to take the oath, they resolved to put him to death on the spot. He had a large family of small children, who, together with his wife, begged that his life might be spared. He himself had no favours to ask of the secessionists. Among his foes, the only point of dispute was, as to the mode of his death. Some favoured shooting, some hanging; but the prevailing majority were in favour of scalding him to death. And there, in the presence of his weeping and helpless family, these fiends in human form *deliberately heated water, with which they scalded to death their chained and defenceless victim.* Thus perished a patriot of whom the State was not worthy. The corpse was then suspended from a tree, with a label on the breast, stating that whoever cut him down and buried him, should suffer the same fate. My companions cut down the corpse by night, and buried it in the forest. May God reward them!

My friend No. 3 thought that it would be best to travel in daylight. He could follow by-paths, and avoid the rebel cavalry. We started about eight o'clock on Friday morning, and met with no incident worth narrating until we reached a mill; here we fell in with some six or seven rebel soldiers, who had been out on sick furlough, and were returning. They scanned us closely, and inquired whence we came, and whither bound. My friend specified a neighbourhood from which he affirmed we came, and stated that we were hunting stray oxen, asking whether they had seen a black ox and a pied ox in their travels. They replied in the negative; and in turn asked him who I was. He replied that I was his wife's brother, who had come from Alabama about three months ago. They said I looked like "death on a pale hoss," and wished to know what was the matter with me—if I were consumptive. My friend replied that I had had the chills for several months; and as there was no quinine in the country, it was impossible to stop them.

During this inquisition, I was ready at any moment to put spur to my horse, and run a race for life, had any attempt been made to arrest me, or if I had been recognised by any of the soldiers. We were, however, permitted to pass on, not without some suspicious glances. We at length reached a point ten miles from Rienzi. My guide now insisted on returning. It would be morning ere he reached home, and if met by cavalry, he must invent some plausible excuse for having a led horse. Nor did he dare return by the same route. Knowing the country, I permitted him to return. I then set out on foot, and at length reached the Federal pickets, three miles from Rienzi, where a horse was furnished me; and about ten o'clock I reached the head-quarters of Colonel Misner in Rienzi. When I gazed upon the star-spangled banner, beneath whose ample folds there was safety and protection—when I saw around me the Union hosts—I shed tears of joy, and from the depths of my heart returned thanks to Almighty God, who had given me my life at my request, preserving me, amid dangers seen and unseen, till I now was safe amid hosts of friends.

Colonel Misner requested me to report all that would be of service to General Rosecrans, which I did, he copying my report as I gave it. I reported, so far as I was informed, the probable number of troops in and around Tupelo, the topography of the country, the probable designs of the rebels, the number of troops sent to Richmond under Beauregard, &c. The Colonel requested me to go with him to headquarters in the morning; but at the hour specified I was sick, and my physician, Dr. Holley, of the Thirty-sixth Illinois, thought it would not be advisable for me to go, even in an ambulance. My report, however, was carried up to General Rosecrans.

Through proper treatment I recovered in a few days, so as to be able to go into Jacinto, the nearest point in the Federal lines to my family. I called on General Jefferson C. Davis, who was in command of that post. The General had heard of my arrest, and expressed gratification at my safe return. I informed him of my desire to get my family within the lines. The General immediately proffered me all the cavalry at his command, and ordered them to prepare for the expedition. I thankfully accepted his kind offer, but after reflection concluded to send a messenger first, with a letter to my wife; if he were not intercepted, I knew that she would come in as soon as possible. The order to the cavalry was countermanded until this plan would be tried. The messenger was not intercepted, and on the next day I had the pleasure of beholding my wife and child, whose faces, a short time before, I had given up all hope of ever beholding on earth.

While here, I called on my friend, Lieutenant Richard Malone, who resides in Jacinto. On inquiring at his house for him, he heard my voice, and ran out to the gate to meet me. Grasping my hand, he could not for some time control his emotions so as to speak.

Malone gave me his history since we had parted at the outer wall of the prison. He reached the corn-field at the point designated, and anxiously awaited my arrival until near daylight, when he was compelled to seek safety in flight. We had agreed to meet in the corn-field at a place where there was a garment suspended upon the fence. We think there must have been two garments suspended at different points, and hence our mistake. We could not signal loud in consequence of the nearness of the pickets, and therefore did not meet. Soon after daylight, Malone found himself in the midst of a cavalry company which had encamped there during the night; they were making preparations for departure, and the majority of them were gathering blackberries. Joining them, he passed as a citizen, and when he reached the rear of the company, he gathered some sticks in his arms, and started towards a small cabin at a short distance, as if it were his residence. Before reaching it, he made a detour to the right, and passed into the dense woods. On the next day, about ten o'clock, A. M., he reached an open champaign country, through which it would have been dangerous to travel. To the west, about three hundred yards distant, was a dense woods, which he hoped to reach without detection. While travelling down a road for this purpose, four cavalrymen who were in pursuit dashed towards him, and ordered him to return with them to Tupelo. Malone replied, that as it was useless to resist, he must submit. He asked for some water; they had none in their canteens, but went to a house in the distance to obtain some. Malone was ordered to march before them, which he was compelled to do, though famishing from hunger and thirst. On reaching the house, they all went to the well and drew a bucket of water. There being no dipper, Malone remarked that he would go into the house and get one. One of the guards followed, and stationed himself at the door with his gun. Malone went into the house, and immediately passed out at the back door. The garden gate being open, he passed into the garden, when he commenced running. Two women in the house noticed his running, and clapping their hands exclaimed, "Your Yankee's gone! Your Yankee's gone!" The guards immediately followed, ordering him to halt, and firing at him with their revolvers. Malone quickly reached a corn-field, and soon after a swamp, whence he made good his escape, and after various vicissitudes reached his family in Jacinto, where I now found him.

I returned to Rienzi with my family, resolved to leave for the North. My wife, before leaving her father's, learned, through a letter sent by a rebel officer to his wife, that all the guards who were on duty during the night I escaped from prison, were placed under close arrest, and were still in the dungeon at the time of his writing. There were eleven guards on each relief, and three reliefs during the night; there were, therefore, thirty-three guards placed under arrest because of my escape.

On the night previous to our departure from Rienzi, we were honoured with a serenade, through the politeness of General Granger, of the cavalry, and Colonel Bryner, of the Forty-seventh Illinois Regiment. Being called on for a speech, I thus responded:

GENTLEMEN—I return you sincere thanks for the honour intended myself and family. In the language of the last tune played by your band, I truly feel at "home again," and it fills my soul with joy to meet my friends once more. What a vast difference a few miles makes! Tupelo is about forty miles south of Rienzi, on an air-line. There I was regarded as a base ingrate, as a despicable traitor, as an enemy to the country, chained as a felon, doomed to die, and before the execution of the sentence, subjected to every species of insult and contumely. Here I meet with the kindest expressions of sympathy from officers of all ranks, from the subaltern to the general, and there is not a private soldier who has heard my tale of woe, who does not manifest a kindly sympathy.

I hope that you will soon pass south of Tupelo; but in your march to the Gulf, may you fare better than I did in my journey to this place. Green corn eaten raw, berries, and stagnant water, would soon cause you to present the emaciated appearance that I do. On your route, call upon the secession sympathizers, and compel them to furnish you with better and more substantial food. My horse I left at Tupelo. He is a valuable animal. The rebel General Hardee, in the true spirit of secession, appropriated—that is, stole—him. However, I did not call to demand him when I left. Being in haste, I did not choose to spare the time, and leaving in the night, I did not wish to disturb the slumbers of the Tupelonians. He is a bright bay. If you meet with him, you may have him for nothing. I would much prefer that he serve the Federal army.

If you take General Jordan prisoner, send me word, and I will furnish you with the iron bands that he put on me, by which you may secure him till he meets the just award of his crimes, which would be death, for destroying the lives of so many Union men.

I hope that you may soon plant the stars and stripes on the shores of the Gulf of Mexico, and play the "Star-spangled Banner" within hearing of its vertiginous billows, after having conquered every foe to the permanence of the glorious Union. I close with the sentiment of the immortal Jackson, which I wish you to bear constantly in mind, in your victorious progress—"The Federal Union—it must and shall be preserved!" Relying upon the God of battles, rest assured that the right cause will triumph, and that after having secured the great object of your warfare, the preservation of the Union, your children and your children's children will rise up and call you blessed, rejoicing in the enjoyment of a free, united, and happy country.

Wishing you abundant success, I beg leave to retire.

On Saturday, the 2d of August, 1862, we left Rienzi, *en route* for the North, in company with William H. Hubbard, Esq., and family, who were also refugees. From the moment I reached the Federal lines I experienced nothing but kindness. I could not mention all who are deserving of thanks from myself and family. I am under special obligations to Generals Nelson, Rosecrans, Granger, Davis, and Asboth; also to Colonel Bryner and Lieutenant Colonel Thrush, of the Forty-seventh Illinois, and Surgeon Lucas, of same regiment, and to Dr. Holley, of the Thirty-sixth Illinois Volunteers; to Josiah King, Esq., of Pittsburgh, Pennsylvania; and Dr. McCook, of Steubenville, Ohio; also Mrs. Ann Wheelwright, of Newburyport, Massachusetts, whose kind letter will ever be remembered, and whose "material aid" entitles her to lasting gratitude; and to Rev. George Potts, D. D., of New York; and Mr. William E. Dubois, of Philadelphia; Rev. Dr. Sprole, Newburgh, New York; Rev. N. Hewitt, D. D., Bridgeport, Connecticut; and Rev. F. N. Ewing, Chicago, Illinois; Rev. J. M. Krebs, D. D., New York; Rev. A. D. Smith, D. D., New York; and Rev. F. Reck Harbaugh, Philadelphia, and many others.

Before closing this chapter I would mention the following incident:

On Wednesday evening, November 19th, I

addressed the citizens of Philadelphia at the Sixth Presbyterian Church, (Rev. F. Reck Harbaugh's.) A report of this address found its way into the city papers. Two days afterwards, while in conversation with Mr. Martien, at his book-store, two soldiers entered, one of whom approached, and thus addressed me;

"Do you know me, sir?"

I replied: "Your face is familiar, but I do not remember your name. It is my misfortune not to be able to remember proper names."

"I read the report of your address in the newspaper, and through the aid of my comrade, I have succeeded in finding you. We have met before, at Tupelo."

At the mention of Tupelo, I immediately recognised in the speaker the man who, after labouring with the others in sundering my chain, engaged the guard, who sat in the doorway, in conversation, while I watched an opportunity to disappear under the prison. Grasping him warmly by the hand, I said: "I now recognise you. You are Mr. Howell Trogdon, of Missouri, late my fellow-prisoner in

Tupelo. How and when did you succeed in leaving that prison?"

"Being a Federal prisoner, I was removed from Tupelo to Mobile, and there parolled on the 26th of August last."

"When was I missed after my escape, and how did the officers act when they learned that I was gone?"

"You were missed at roll-call, the next morning, and in a short time, many officers came into the prison. They were greatly enraged at this, your second flight. The prisoners were closely questioned as to their complicity in your escape, but they denied all knowledge of the matter. Soon all the prison-guards on duty during the night, thirty-three in number, were brought into the prison in chains. The cavalry was ordered out in search of you, and directed to shoot you down where-ever found. The mode of your escape was not discovered, and the officers were of the opinion that you had bribed the guards. *From that time, the officers became more cruel than ever, and in two weeks, thirty-two of our fellow-prisoners were taken out and shot!* We never learned whether you had succeeded in escaping to the Union lines. We feared that you were overtaken and shot, or that you perished in the swamps from hunger, thirst, and fatigue. I hope soon to see McHatten, Speer, De Grummond, and Soper, who are also parolled, and they will rejoice to learn that you still live. During the night of your escape, we slept but little, through fear that *our chaplain* might be shot by the guards, and I assure you many fervent prayers ascended to Heaven for your safety."

# CHAPTER VII.

## SOUTHERN CLASSES—CRUELTY TO SLAVES.

**Sandhillers—Dirt-eating—Dipping—Their Mode of Living—Patois—Rain-book—Wife-trade—Coming in to see the Cars—Superstition—Marriage of Kinsfolks—Hardshell Sermon—Causes which lead to the Degradation of this Class—Efforts to Reconcile the Poor Whites to the Peculiar Institution—The Slaveholding Class—The Middle Class—Northern Isms—Incident at a Methodist Minister's House—Question asked a Candidate for Licensure—Reason of Southern Hatred toward the North—Letter to Mr. Jackman—Barbarities and Cruelties of Slavery—Mulattoes—Old Cole—Child Born at Whipping-post—Advertisement of a Keeper of Bloodhounds—Getting Rid of Free Blacks—The Doom of Slavery—Methodist Church South.**

The sojourner in the Slave States is struck with the wretched and degraded appearance of a class of people called by the slaveholders, "poor white folks," and "the tallow-faced gentry," from their pallid complexion. They live in wretched hovels, dress slatternly, and are exceedingly filthy in their habits. Many of them are clay or dirt-eaters, which is said to cause their peculiar complexion. Their children, at a very early age, form this filthy and disgusting habit; and mere infants may be found with their mouths filled with dirt. The mud with which they daub the interstices between the logs of their rude domicils, must be frequently renewed, as the occupants pick it all out in a very short time, and eat it. This pernicious practice induces disease. The complexion becomes pale, similar to that occasioned by chronic ague and fever.

Akin to this is the practice of snuff-dipping, which is not confined exclusively to females of the poor white caste, though scarcely one in fifty of this class is exempt from the disgusting habit. The method is this: The female snuff-dipper takes a short stick, and wetting it with her saliva, dips it into her snuff-box, and then rubs the gathered dust all about her mouth, and into the interstices of her teeth, where she allows it to remain until its strength has been fully absorbed. Others hold the stick thus loaded with snuff in the cheek, *a la quid* of tobacco, and suck it with a decided relish, while engaged in their ordinary avocations;

while others simply fill the mouth with the snuff, and imitate, to all intents and purposes, the chewing propensities of the men. In the absence of snuff, tobacco in the plug or leaf is invariably resorted to as a substitute. Oriental betel-chewing, and the Japanese fashion of blacking the teeth of married ladies, are the height of elegance compared with snuff-dipping. The habit leads to a speedy decay of the teeth, and to nervous disorders of every kind. Those who indulge in it become haggard at a very early age.

The *Petersburg* (Va.) *Express* estimates the number of women in that State as one hundred and twenty-five thousand, one hundred thousand of whom are snuff-dippers. Every five of these will use a two-ounce paper of snuff per day; that is, to the hundred thousand dippers, two thousand five hundred pounds a day, amounting, in one year, to the enormous quantity of nine hundred and twelve thousand pounds. This practice prevails generally, it says, among the poor whites, though some females of the higher classes are guilty of it.

The poor whites obtain their subsistence, as far as practicable, in the primitive aboriginal mode, viz., by hunting and fishing. When these methods fail to afford a supply, they cultivate a truck-patch, and some of them raise a bale or two of cotton, with the proceeds of the sale of which they buy whiskey, tobacco, and a few necessary articles. When all other methods fail, they resort to stealing, to which many of them are addicted from choice, as well as from necessity. They are exceeding slovenly in their habits, cleanliness being a rare virtue. Indolence is a prevailing vice, and its lamentable effects are everywhere visible. They fully obey the scriptural injunction, take no thought for the morrow. A present supply, sufficient to satisfy nature's most urgent demands, being obtained, their care ceases, and they relapse into listless inactivity. They herd together upon the poor sand-hills, the refuse land of the country, which the rich slaveholder will not purchase, for which reason, they are sometimes called sand-hillers, and here they live, and their children, and their children's children, through successive generations, in the same deplorable condition of wretchedness and degradation.

They are exceedingly ignorant; not one adult in fifty can write; not one in twenty can read. They can scarcely be said to speak the English language, using a patois which is scarcely intelligible. An old lady thus related an incident of which her daughter "*Sal*" was the heroine. "My darter Sal yisterday sot the lather to the damsel tree, and clim up, and knocked some of the nicest saftest damsels I ever seed in my born days." I once called to make some inquiry about the road, at a small log tenement, inhabited by a sand-hiller and family. A sheet was hanging upon the wall, containing the portraits of the Presidents of the United States. I remarked to the lady of the house that those were, I believed, the pictures of the Presidents.

"Yes!" she replied; "they is, and I've hearn tell of 'em a long time. They must be gittin' mighty old, ef some of 'em aint dead. That top one," she continued, "is Gineral Washington. I've hearn of him ever sence I was a gal.

He must be gittin' up in years, ef he aint dead. Him and Gineral Jackson fit the British and Tories at New Orleans, and whipped 'em, too."

She seemed to pride herself greatly on her historical knowledge.

One of these geniuses once informed me of a peculiar kind of book "he'd hearn tell on," that the Yankees had. He had forgotten its name, but thus described it: "It told the day of the week the month come in on. It told when we was a gwine to have rain, and what kind of wether we was gwine to have in gineral. May-be they call it a rain-book."

I replied that I had heard of the book, and I believed that it was called an Almanac.

"You've said it now," remarked the man. "It's a alminick, and I'd give half I's wuth to have one. I'd no when to take a umberell, and if I haddent nary one, I'd no when I could go a huntin' without gittin' wet."

Two of these semi-savages had resolved to remove to the West, in hope of bettering their condition. One wished to remove to Arkansas, the other to Texas. The wife of the former

19

wished to go to Texas, the latter to Arkansas. The husbands were desirous of gratifying their spouses, but could devise no plan that seemed likely to prove satisfactory, till one day when hunting, finding game scarce, they sat down upon a log, when the following dialogue took place:

"Kit, I'm sort o' pestered about Dilsie. She swars to Rackensack she'll go, and no whar else. I allers had a hankerin' arter Texas. Plague take Rackensack, I say! Ef a man war thar, the ager and the airthquakes ed shake him out on it quicker en nothin'."

"When a woman's set on a gwine anywhar, they're a gwine. It's jest no use to talk. I've coaxed Minnie more'n a little to go long with me to Arkansas, and the more I coax, the more she wont go."

"Well, Kit, 'sposen we swap women."

"Well, Sam, what trade'll ye gin?"

"Oh! a gentleman's trade, of course!"

"Shucks, Sam! 'sposen I had a young filly, and you a old mar, ye wouldn't ax an even trade, would ye?"

"No; it 'ud be too hard. I tell you what I'll do, Kit. Here's a shot-gun that's wuth ten dollars, ef it's wuth a red. I'll give it and that ar b'ar-skin hangin' on the side of my shanty, to boot, and say it's a trade."

"Nuff sed, ef the women's agreed."

Home they went, and stated the case to the women, who, *after due deliberation*, acceded to the proposition, having also made a satisfactory arrangement about the children, and they all soon went on their way rejoicing to their respective destinations in that

> "American's haven of eternal rest,
> Found a little farther West."

On the Sabbath after the completion of the Memphis and Charleston railroad, a large number of the sand-hillers came to Iuka Springs, to witness the passing of the cars. Arriving too early, they visited a church where divine service was progressing. Whilst the minister was in the midst of his sermon, the locomotive whistle sounded, when a stampede took place to the railroad. The exodus left the parson almost alone in his glory. The passing train caused the most extravagant expressions and gestures of wonder and astonishment by these rude observers. It was an era in their life.

Once while standing on the railroad-track, I observed a crowd of these people coming to see the *"elephant."* They came so near, that I overheard their conversation. One young lass, of sweet sixteen, with slattern dress and dishevelled hair, looking up the road, which was visible for a great distance, thus expressed her astonishment at what she saw: "O, dad! what a long piece of iron!" Soon the whistle sounded; this they had never heard before, and came to the conclusion that it was a dinner-horn. As soon as the cars came in sight, they scattered like frightened sheep, some on one side of the road, and some on the other. Nor did they halt till they had placed fifty yards at least between them and the track.

Superstition prevails amongst them to a fearful extent. Almost every hut has a horse-shoe nailed above the door, or on the threshold, to keep out witches. In sickness, charms and incantations are used to drive away disease. Their physicians are chiefly what are termed faith-doctors, who are said to work miraculous cures. They are strong believers in luck. If a rabbit cross their path, they will turn round to change their luck. If, on setting out on a journey, an owl hoot on the left hand, they will return and set out anew. If the new moon is seen through brush, or on the left hand, it is a bad omen. They will have trouble during the lunar month. When the whippoorwill is first heard in the spring, they turn head over heels thrice, to prevent back-ache during the year. Dreams are harbingers of joy or wo. To dream of snakes, is ominous. To dream of seeing a coffin, or conversing with the dead, is a sign of approaching dissolution, and many have no doubt perished through terror, occasioned by such dreams. Fortune-tellers are rife amongst them—those sages whose comprehensive view knows the past, the present, and the future. They seek unto familiar spirits, that peep and mutter, for the living to the dead.

They have many deformed, and blind, and deaf among them, in consequence of the intermarriage of relatives. Cousins often marry, and occasionally they marry within the degrees of consanguinity prohibited by the law of God. Perhaps this divine law forbids the marriage of cousins when it declares, "Thou shalt not marry any that is near of kin." The sad effects on posterity, both mentally and physically, lead to the conviction that if the law of God does not condemn it, physiological law does.

These sand-hillers do not (when no serious preventive occurs) fail to attend the elections, where the highest bidder obtains their vote. Sometimes their vote will command cash, and sometimes only whiskey. It is sad to witness the elective franchise, that highest and most glorious badge of a freeman, thus prostituted.

The proverb holds good—Like people, like priest. Their ministers are ignorant, ranting fanatics. They despise literature, and every Sabbath fulminate censures upon an educated ministry. The following is a specimen of their preaching. Mr. V—— is a Hard-shell Baptist, or, as they term themselves, "Primitive Baptists." Entering the pulpit on a warm morning in July, he will take off his coat and vest, roll up his sleeves, and then begin:

MY BRETHERING AND SISTERN—I air a ignorant man, follered the plough all my life, and never rubbed agin nary college. As I said afore, I'm ignorant, and I thank God for it. (Brother Jones responds, "Passon, yer ort to be very thankful, fur yer very ignorant.") Well, I'm agin all high larnt fellers what preaches grammar and Greek fur a thousand dollars a year They preaches fur the money, and they gits it, and that's all they'll git. They've got so high larnt they contradicts Scripter, what plainly tells us that the sun rises and sets. They seys it don't, but that the yerth whirls round, like clay to the seal. What ud cum of the water in the wells ef it did. Wodent it all spill out, and leave 'em dry, and whar ed we be? I may say to them, as the sarpent said unto David, much learning hath made thee mad.

When I preaches, I never takes a tex till I goes inter the pulpit; then I preaches a plain sarment, what even women can understand. I never premedertates, but what is given to me in that same hour, that I sez. Now I'm a gwine ter open the Bible, and the first verse I sees, I'm a gwine to take it for a tex. (Suiting the action to the word, he opened the Bible, and commenced reading and spelling together.) Man is f-e-a-r-f-u-l-l-y—fearfully—and w-o-n-d-e-r-f-u-l-l-y—wonderfully — m-a-d-e — mad.— "Man is fearfully and wonderfully made." (Pronounced *mad.*) Well, it's a quar tex, but I said I's a gwine to preach from it, and I'm a gwine to do it. In the fust place, I'll divide my sarment into three heads. Fust and foremost, I show you that a man will git mad. 2d. That sometimes he'll git fearfully mad; and thirdly and lastly, when thar's lots of things to vex and pester him, he'll git fearfully and wonderfully mad. And in the application I'll show you that good men sometimes gits mad, for the Posle David hisself, who rote the tex, got mad, and called all men liars, and cussed his enemies, wishen' 'em to go down quick into hell; and Noah, he got tite, and cussed his nigger boy Ham, just like some drunken masters now cusses their niggers. But Noah and David repented; and all on us what gits mad must repent, or the devil 'll git us.

Thus he ranted, to the great edification of his hearers, who regard him as a perfect Boanerges, to which title his stentorian voice would truly entitle him. This exordium will serve as a specimen of the "sarment," as it continued in the same strain to the end of the peroration.

Where there is no vision, the people perish. Such blind leaders of the blind are liable, with their infatuated followers, to fall into a ditch worse than Bunyan's Slough of Despond. This minister had undoubtedly run when he was not sent, though he "had hearn a call; a audible voice had, while he was a shucken corn, said unto him, Preach." Though God does not need men's learning, yet he has as little use for their ignorance. Learning is the handmaid of religion, but must not be substituted in its stead.

The causes which induce this "wilderness of mind" are patent to all who make even a cursory examination. There is a tendency in the poor to ape the manners of the rich. Those having slaves to labour in their stead, toil not physically; hence labour falls into disrepute, and the poorer classes, having no slaves to work for them, and not choosing to submit to the degradation of labour, incur all the evils resulting from idleness and poverty. Ignorance and vice of every kind soon ensue, and a general apathy prevails, which destroys in a great measure all mental and physical vigour.

The slaveholders buy up all the fertile lands to be cultivated by their slaves; hence the poor are crowded out, and if they remain in the vicinity of the place of their nativity, they must occupy the poor tracts whose sterility does not excite the cupidity of their rich neighbours. The slaveholders' motto is, "Let us buy more negroes to raise more cotton, to buy more negroes, and so on *ad infinitum.* To raise more cotton they must also buy more land. Small farmers are induced to sell out to them, and move further west. For this reason, the white population of the fertile sections of the older slave States is constantly on the decrease, while the slave population is as constantly increasing. Thus the slaveholder often acquires many square miles of land, and hundreds of human chattels. He is, as it were, set alone in the earth. Priding himself upon his wealth, he will not send his princely sons to the same school with the poor white trash; he either sends them to some distant college or seminary, or employs a private teacher exclusively for his children. The poor whites in the neighbourhood, even should they desire to educate their children, have no means to pay for their tuition. Compelled to live on poor or worn-out lands, honest toil considered degrading, and forced to submit to many inconveniences and disabilities (all the offices of honour and profit being monopolized by the slaveholders,) through the workings of the "peculiar institution," they find it utterly impossible to educate their offspring, even in the rudiments of their mother tongue. As the power of slavery increases, their condition waxes worse and worse.

The slaveocracy becomes more exacting. Laws are passed by the legislature compelling non-slaveholders to patrol the country nightly, to prevent insurrections by the negroes. They denounce the law, but coercion is resorted to, and the poor whites are forced to obey. When their masters call for them, they must leave their labour, by day or by night, patrol the country, follow the bloodhounds, arrest the fugitive slave, and do all other dirty work which their tyrants demand. If they refuse to obey, they are denounced as abolitionists, and are in danger of death at the hands of Judge Lynch, the mildest punishment they can hope for being a coat of tar and feathers.

The house-negroes feel themselves several degrees above the poor whites, as they, from their opportunities for observation amongst the higher classes, are possessed of greater information and less rusticity than this less favoured class. The poor whites have no love for the institution of slavery. They regard it as the instrument of inflicting upon them many wrongs, and depriving them of many rights. They dare not express their sentiments to the slaveholders, who hold them completely under their power. A. G. Brown, United States Senator from Mississippi, to reconcile the poor whites to the peculiar institution, used the following arguments in a speech at Iuka Springs, Mississippi. He stated, that if the slaves were liberated, and suffered to remain in the country, the rich would have money to enable them to go to some other clime, and that the poor whites would be compelled to remain amongst the negroes, who would steal their property, and destroy their lives; and if slavery were abolished, and the negroes removed and colonized, the rich would take the poor whites for slaves, in their stead, and reduce them to the condition of the Irish and Dutch in the North, whose condition he represented to be one of cruel bondage. These statements had some effect upon his auditors, who believed, from sad experience, that the rich could oppress the poor as they chose, and might, in the contingency specified, reduce them to slavery. Labour is considered so degrading, that any argument, based upon making labour compulsory on their part, has its weight. Even the beggar despises work. A sturdy beggar asked alms at a house at which I was lodging. As he appeared to be a man of great physical strength, he was advised to go to work, and thus provide for his wants. "Work!" said he, in disgust; "niggers do the work in this country"—and retired highly insulted.

This people form a distinct class, distinguished by as many characteristics from the middle and higher classes of Southern society, as the Jews are from the nations amongst whom they sojourn. The causes which brought about their reduction to their present state of semi-barbarism, must be removed, ere they can rise to the condition whence they have fallen. They must rise upon the ruins of slavery. When the peculiar institution is abolished, then, and not till then, will their disabilities be removed, and they be in reality what they are nominally—freemen.

Slaveholders and their families form a distinct class, characterized by idleness, vanity, licentiousness, profanity, dissipation, and tyranny. There are glorious exceptions, it is true, but those are the distinguishing traits of the class. The middle class is the virtuous class of the South. They are industrious, frugal, hospitable, simple in their habits, plain and unostentatious in their manners. Some of this class are small slaveholders, but the great majority own none. The gross vices of the higher class are not found among them. They labour regardless of the sneers of their aristocratic neighbours. Senator Hammond, of South Carolina, may call them mudsills; they regard it not, but pursue the even tenor of their way. The slow, unmoving finger of scorn may be pointed at them by the sons of pride, yet they refuse to eat the bread of idleness, and labour with their *own hands*, that they may provide things honest in the sight of all men. Equidistant from poverty and riches, they enjoy the golden mean, and immunity from the temptations incident to the extremes of abject poverty and great riches.

In the slave States all those born north of the "nigger line," are denominated Yankees. This is applied as a term of reproach. When a southerner is angry with a man of northern nativity, he does not fail to stigmatize him as a Yankee. The slaveholders manifest considerable antipathy against the Yankees, which has been increasing during the last ten years. In 1858, the Legislature of Mississippi passed resolutions recommending non-intercourse with the "Abolition States," and requesting the people not to patronize natives of those States residing amongst them, and especially to discountenance Yankee ministers and teachers. In the educational notice of Memphis Synodical College, at La Grange, Tennessee, it is expressly stated that the Faculty are of southern birth and education. The principals of the Female Seminaries at Corinth and Iuka, Mississippi, give notice that no Yankee teachers will be employed in those institutions. While on a visit at the house of a Methodist clergyman, quite a number of ministers, returning from Conference, called to tarry for the night. During the evening, one of them, learning that I was "*Yankee born,*" thus interrogated me: "Why is it, sir, that all kinds of delusions originate in the North, such as Millerism, Mormonism, Spirit-rappings, and Abolitionism?" To which I replied: "The North originates everything. All the text-books used in southern schools, all the books on law, physic, and divinity, are written and published north of Mason & Dixon's line. The South does not even print Bibles. The magnetic telegraph, the locomotive, Lucifer matches, and even the cotton-gin, are all northern inventions. The South, sir, has not sense enough to invent a decent humbug. These humbugs once originated, the South is always well represented by believers in them. I have known more men to go from this county (Shelby county, Tennessee) to the Mormons, than I have known to go from the whole State of Ohio."

When I had thus spoken, my inquisitor was nonplussed, and the laugh went against him.

When a candidate before the Presbytery of Chickasaw, in Mississippi, for licensure, one of the members of Presbytery, learning that I was a "Yankee," asked me the following questions, and received the following answers:

"Mr. Aughey, when will the day of judgment take place?"

"The Millerites have stated that the 30th of June next will be the judgment-day. As for myself, I have had no revelation on the subject, and expect none."

"Do you believe that any one can call the spirits?"

"I do, sir."

"What! believe that the spirits can be called?"

"I do, sir."

"I will vote, then, against your licensure, if you have fallen into this heresy of the land of your nativity."

Another then said:

"Brother Aughey, please explain yourself.

I know you do not believe in spirit-rapping."

"I do not, sir, though I believe, as I stated, that any one may call the spirits; but I do not believe that they will come in answer to the call."

A lady once remarked to me that she did not believe that a northern man would ever become fully reconciled to the institution of slavery, and that his influence and sentiments, whatever might be his profession of attachment to the peculiar institution, would be against it. The cause of the general opposition to northern men is their opposition to slavery. Their testimony is against its abominations and barbarities, and hence the wish to impair the credibility of the witnesses.

An illustration of the working of the institution may be found in the following letter:

KOSCIUSKO, ATTALA COUNTY, MISSISSIPPI,<br>December 25, 1861.

MR. WILLIAM JACKMAN:

*Dear Sir*—Your last kind and truly welcome letter came to hand in due course of mail. I owe you an apology for delaying an answer so long. My apparent neglect was occasioned by no want of respect for you; but in consequence of the disturbed state of the country, and difficulty of communication with the North, I feared my reply would never reach you. Now, however, by directing "*via* Norfolk and flag of truce," letters are sent across the lines to the North. In your letter you desired me, from this stand-point, to give you my observations of the workings of the peculiar institution, and an expression of my views as to its consistency with the eternal principles of rectitude and justice. In reply, I will give you a plain narrative of facts.

On my advent to the South, I was at first struck with the fact that the busy hum of labour had in some measure ceased. What labour I did observe progressing, was done with little skill, and mainly by negroes. I called upon the Rev. Dr. R. J. Breckinridge, to whom I had a letter of introduction, who treated me with the greatest kindness, inviting me to make his house my home when I visited that section of country. On leaving his house, he gave me some directions as to the road I must travel to reach a certain point. "You will pass," said he, "a blacksmith's shop, where a one-eyed man is at work—my property." The phrase, "my property," I had never before heard applied to a human being, and though I had never been taught to regard the relation of master and slave as a sinful relation, yet it grated harshly upon my ears to hear a human being, a tradesman, called a chattel; but it grated much more harshly, a week after this, to hear the groans of two such chattels, as they underwent a severe flagellation, while chained to the whipping-post, because they had, by half an hour, overstayed their time with their families on an adjoining plantation.

The next peculiar abomination of the peculiar institution which I observed, was the licentiousness engendered by it. Mr. D. T——, of Madison county, Kentucky, had a white family of children, and a black, or rather mulatto family. As his white daughters married, he gave each a mulatto half-sister, as a waiting-girl, or body-servant. Mr. K——, of Winchester, Kentucky, had a mulatto daughter, and he was also the father of her child, thus re-enacting Lot's sin. Dr. C——, of Tishomingo county, Mississippi, has a negro concubine, and a white servant to wait on her. Mr. B——, of Marshall county, Mississippi, lived with his white wife till he had grandchildren, some of whom came to school to me, when he repudiated his white wife, and attached himself to a very homely old African, who superintends his household, and rules his other slaves with rigour. Mr. S——, of Tishomingo county, Mississippi, has a negro concubine, and a large family of mulatto children. He once brought this woman to church in Rienzi, to the great indignation of the white ladies, who removed to a respectable distance from her.

I preached recently to a large congregation of slaves, the third of whom were as white as myself. Some of them had red hair and blue eyes. If there are any marked characteristics of their masters' families, the mulatto slaves are possessed of these characteristics. I refer to physical peculiarities, such as large mouths, humped shoulders, and peculiar expressions of countenance. I asked a gentleman how it happened that some of his slaves had red hair. He replied that he had a red-headed overseer for several years.

I never knew a pious overseer—never! There may be many, but I never saw one. Overseers, as a class, are worse than slaveholders themselves. They are cruel, brutal, licentious, dissipated, and profane. They always carry a loaded whip, a revolver, and a Bowie-knife. These men have the control of women, whom they often whip to death. Mr. P——, who resided near Holly Springs, had a negro woman whipped to death while I was at his house during a session of Presbytery. Mr. C——, of Waterford, Mississippi, had a woman whipped to death by his overseer. But such cruel scourgings are of daily occurrence. Colonel H——, a member of my church, told me yesterday that he ordered a boy, who he supposed was *feigning* sickness, to the whipping-post, but that he had not advanced ten steps toward it, when he fell dead!—and the servant was free from his master. During our conversation, a girl passed. "There is a girl," said he, "who does not look very white in the face, owing to exposure; but when I strip her to whip her, I find that she has a skin as fair as my wife." Mrs. F—— recently whipped a boy to death within half a mile of my residence. A jury of inquest returned a verdict that he came to his death by cruelty; but nothing more was done. Mrs. M—— and her daughter, of Holly Springs, abused a girl repeatedly. She showed her bruises to some of my acquaintances, and they believed them fatal. She soon after died. Mr. S——, a member of my church, has several maimed negroes from abuse on the part of the overseer.

I am residing on the banks of the Yock-a-nookany, which means "meandering," when translated from the Indian tongue. In this vicinity there are large plantations, cultivated by hundreds of negroes. The white population is sparse. Every night the negroes are brought to a judgment-seat. The overseer presides.

If they have not laboured to suit him, or if their task is unfulfilled, they are chained to a post, and severely whipped. The victims are invariably stripped; to what extent, is at the option of the overseer. In Louisiana, women, preparatory to whipping, are often stripped to a state of perfect nudity. Old Mr. C——, of Waterford, Mississippi, punished his negroes *by slitting the soles of their feet with his Bowie-knife!* One man he put into a cotton-press, and turned the screw till life was extinct. He stated that he only intended to alarm the man, but carried the joke too far. I have heard women thus plead, in piteous accents, when chained to the whipping-post, and stripped: "O, my God, master! don't whip me! I was sick! indeed I was sick! I had a chill, and the fever is on me now! I haven't tasted a morsel to-day! You know I works when I is well! O for God's sake don't whip a poor sick nigger! My poor chile's sick too! Missis thinks it's a dyin'! O master, for the love of God, don't cut a poor distressed woman wid your whip! I'll try to do better, ef you'll only let me off this once!" These piteous plaints only rouse the ire of their cruel task-masters, who sometimes knock them down in the midst of their pleadings. I have known an instance of a woman giving birth to a child at the whipping-post. The fright and pain brought on premature labour.

One beautiful Sabbath morning I stood on the levee at Baton Rouge, Louisiana, and counted twenty-seven sugar-houses in full blast. I found that the negroes were compelled to labour eighteen hours per day, and were not permitted to rest on the Sabbath during the rolling season. The negroes on most plantations have a truck-patch, which they cultivate on the Sabbath. I have pointed out the sin of thus labouring on the Sabbath, but they plead necessity; their children, they state, must suffer from hunger if they did not cultivate their truck-patch, and their masters would not give them time on any other day.

Negroes, by law, are prohibited from learning to read. This law was not strictly enforced in Tennessce and some other States till within a few years past. I had charge of a Sabbath-school for the instruction of blacks in Memphis, Tennessee, in 1853. This school was put down by the strong arm of the law in a short time after my connection with it ceased. In Mississippi, a man who taught slaves to read or write would be sent to the penitentiary instanter. The popular plea for this wickedness is, that if they were taught to read, they would read abolition documents; and if they were taught to write, they would write themselves passes, and pass northward to Canada.

Such advertisements as the following often greet the eye.

"*Kansas War.*—The undersind taks this method of makkin it noan that he has got a pack of the best nigger hounds in the South. My hounds is well trand, and I has had much experience a huntin niggers, having follered it for the last fiften year. I will go anywhar that I'm sent for, and will ketch niggers at the follerin raits.

"My raits fur ketchin runaway niggers $10 per hed, ef they's found in the beat whar thar master lives; $15 if they's found in the county, and $50 if they's tuck out on the county.

"N. B.—Pay is due when the nigger is tuck. Planters ort to send fur me as soon as thar niggers runs away, while thar trak is fresh."

Every night the woods resound with the deep-mouthed baying of the bloodhounds. The slaves are said by some to love their masters; but it requires the terrors of bloodhounds and the fugitive slave law to keep them in bondage. You in the North are compelled to act the part of the bloodhounds here, and catch the fugitives for the planters of the South. Free negroes are sold into bondage for the most trivial offences. Slaveholders declare that the presence of free persons of colour exerts a pernicious influence upon their slaves, rendering them discontented with their condition, and inspiring a desire for freedom. They therefore are very desirous of getting rid of these persons, either by banishing them from the State or enslaving them. The legislature of Mississippi has passed a law for their expulsion, and other States have followed in the wake. The Governor of Missouri has vetòed the law for the expulsion of free persons of cólour, passed by the legislature of that State because of its unconstitutionality.

Were I to recount all the abominations of the peculiar institution, and the wrongs inflicted upon the African race, that have come under my observation, they would fill a large volume. Slavery is guilty of six abominations; yea, seven may justly be charged upon it. It is said that the negro is lazy, and will not work except by compulsion. I have known negroes who have purchased their freedom by the payment of a large sum, and afterward made not only a good living, but a fortune beside. It is said Judge W—— of South Carolina gave his servants the use of his plantation, upon condition that they would support his family; and that in three years he was compelled to take the management himself, as they did not make a comfortable living for themselves and the Judge's family. In reply, it might be said that the negroes had not a fair trial, as no one had any property he could call his own, and they were thrown into a sort of Fourierite society, having all things in common. In this state of things, while some would work, others would be idle. White men do not succeed in such communities, and for this reason it was no fair test of the industrial energies of Judge W——'s slaves.

The question is often asked, is slavery sinful in itself? My observation has been extensive, embracing eight slave States, and I have never yet seen any example of slavery that I did not deem sinful. If slavery is not sinful in itself, I must have always seen it out of itself. I have observed its workings during eleven years, amongst a professedly Christian people, and cannot do otherwise than pronounce it an unmitigated curse. It is a curse to the white man, it is a curse to the black man. That God will curse it, and blot it out of existence ere long, is my firm conviction. The elements of its abolition exist; God speed the time when they will be fully developed, and this mother of abominations driven from the land of the free! The development of the eternal principles of justice and rectitude will abolish this hoary monster of fraud and oppression. Slavery subverts all the rights of man. It divests him of citizenship, of liberty, of the pursuit of happiness, of his children, of his wife, of his property, of intellectual culture, reserving to him only the rights of the horse and ass, and reducing him to the same chattel condition with them. Not a single right does the State law grant him above that of the mule —no, not one. The chastity of the slave has no legal protection. The Methodist Church South is expunging from the discipline everything inimical to the peculiar institution, whilst I observe that the Church North is adding to her testimony and deliverances against the sin of slaveholding. The Church South refused to abide by the rules of the Church, and hence the guilt of the schism lies with her, and you are henceforth free from any guilt in conniving at the sin which the founder of your church, the illustrious Wesley, regarded as the "sum of all villany."

Remember me kindly to Mrs. Jackman and

family. Hoping to hear from you soon, I beg leave to subscribe myself,

Yours fraternally,

JOHN H. AUGHEY.

To Mr. William Jackman,
Amsterdam, Jefferson Co., Ohio.

# CHAPTER VIII.

## NOTORIOUS REBELS.—UNION OFFICERS.

**Colonel Jefferson Davis—His Speech at Holly Springs, Mississippi—His Opposition to Yankee Teachers and Ministers—A bid for the Presidency—His Ambition—Burr, Arnold, Davis.—General Beauregard—Headquarters at Rienzi—Colonel Elliott's Raid—Beauregard's Consternation—Personal description—His illness—Popularity waning.—Rev. Dr. Palmer of New Orleans—His influence—The Cincinnati Letter—His Personal Appearance—His Denunciations of General Butler—His Radicalism.—Rev. Dr. Waddell of La Grange, Tennessee—His Prejudices against the North—President of Memphis Synodical College—His Talents prostituted.—Union Officers—General Nelson—General Sherman.**

### COLONEL JEFFERSON DAVIS.

In 1856 I heard Colonel Jefferson Davis deliver an address at Holly Springs, Mississippi. The Colonel is about a medium height, of slender frame, his nose aquiline, his hair dark, his manners polite. He is no orator. His speech was principally a tirade of abuse against the North, bitterly inveighing against the emigrant aid societies which had well-nigh put Kansas upon the list of free States. He advised the people to employ no more Yankee teachers. He had been educated in the North, and he regarded it as the greatest misfortune of his life. Soon after Colonel Davis visited New England, where he eulogized that section in an extravagant manner. He was pleased with everything he saw; even "Noah Webster's Yankee spelling-book" received a share of the Colonel's fulsome flattery. On his return to the South, "a change came o'er the spirit of his dream," and his bile and bitterness against Yankee-land returned in all its pristine vigour. The Colonel was making a bid for the Presidency; but New England was not so easily gulled; his flimsy professions of friendship were too transparent to hide the hate which lay beneath, and his aspirations were doomed to disappointment.

Though Colonel Davis is often called Mississippi's pet, yet he is not regarded as a truthful man, and his reports and messages are received with considerable abatement by "the chivalry." His ambition knows no bounds. He would rather "reign in hell than serve in heaven."

Had Jefferson Davis been elected President of the United States, he would have been among the last instead of the first to favour secession. Had he been slain on the bloody fields of Mexico, his memory would have been cherished. History will assign him a place among the infamous. Burr, Arnold, and Davis will be names for ever execrated by true patriots. The two former died a natural death, though the united voice of their countrymen would have approved of their execution on the gallows. The fate of the latter lies still in the womb of futurity, though his loyal countrymen, without a dissenting voice, declare that he deserves a felon's doom. An announcement of his death would suffuse no patriot's eye with tears. What loyalist would weep while he read the news-item—the arch traitor Jeff. Davis is dead.

## GENERAL G. T. BEAUREGARD.

I met General Beauregard under very peculiar circumstances. I had gone to Rienzi for the purpose of escaping to the Federal lines for protection from the rigorous and sweeping conscript law. When I arrived, I found the rebels evacuating Corinth, and their sick and wounded passing down the Mobile and Ohio railroad to the hospitals below. General Beauregard had just arrived in Rienzi, and had his headquarters at the house of Mr. Sutherland. A rumour had spread through Rienzi that General Beauregard had ordered the women and children to leave the town. Many of them, believing that the order had been issued, were hastening into the country. In order to confirm or refute the statement, I called upon General Beauregard, and asked him whether he had issued such an order. He replied, "I have issued no such order, sir." Just at that moment a courier arrived with the information that the Yankees had attacked the advance of their retreating army at Boonville, that they had destroyed the depot, and taken many prisoners. The General told the courier that he must be mistaken; that it was impossible for the Yankees to pass around his army. While he was yet speaking a citizen arrived from Boonville, confirming the statement of the courier. Beauregard was still incredulous, replying that they must have mistaken the Confederates for the Yankees. In a few minutes the explosion of shells shook the building. The General then thought that it might be true that the Yankees had passed around the army; but on hearing the shells, he stated that General Green (of Missouri) was driving them away with his cannon. The truth was soon ascertained by the arrival of several couriers. Col. Elliott, of the Federal army, had made a raid upon Boonville, had fired the depot, and destroyed a large train of cars filled with ammunition. The explosions of the shells which we heard was occasioned by the fire reaching the cars in which these shells were stored. The Colonel also destroyed the railroad to such an extent that it required several days to repair the track.

General Beauregard is below the medium height, and has a decidedly French expression of countenance. His hair is quite gray, though a glance at his face will convince the observer that it is prematurely so. The General is regarded as taciturn. His countenance is careworn and haggard. During the winter of 1861–2, he was attacked with bronchitis and typhoid pneumonia, and came near dying; and had not, at my interview, by any means recovered his pristine health and vigour. His prestige as an able commander is rapidly waning. For some time his military talents were considered of the first order; now a third-rate position is assigned him. He is still regarded as a first-class engineer. When General Sterling Price arrived at Corinth, General Beauregard conducted him around all the fortifications, explaining their nature and unfolding their strength; but no word of approval could he elicit from the Missouri General. At length he ventured to ask what he thought of their capacity for resisting an attack. General Price replied, "They may prove effective in resisting an attack. These are the second fortifications I ever saw; the first I captured." He had reference to Colonel Mulligan's, at Lexington, Missouri. Sumter and Manassas gave Beauregard fame. Since the latter battle his star has declined steadily; and if the Federal generals prove themselves competent, it will soon go out in total darkness, and the world's verdict will be, it was a misfortune that Beauregard lived.

## REV. DR. B. M. PALMER.

Dr. Palmer has done more than any non-combatant in the South to promote the rebellion. He was accessory both before and after the fact. His sermons are nearly all abusive of the North. The mudsills of Yankeedom and the scum of Europe are phrases of frequent use in his public addresses, and they are meant to include all living north of what is more familiarly than elegantly termed in the South the "nigger line," although the North is the land of his parental nativity.

A few years ago, Dr. Palmer wrote to a friend in Cincinnati respecting a vacant church, in which he gave as one reason, among others, for desiring to come North, that he wished to remove his family from the baleful influences of slavery. That letter still exists, and ought to be published.

Dr. Palmer's personal appearance is by no means prepossessing. He is small of stature, of very dark complexion, dish-faced. His nose is said to have been bròken when a child; at all events, it is a deformity. He is fluent in speech, has a vivid imagination, and has a great influence over a promiscuous congregation.

After the reduction of Forts Jackson and St. Philip, and the capture of New Orleans, Dr. Palmer came to Corinth, where he preached to the rebel army. His text was invariably General Butler's "women-of-the-town order," which we fully believe he intentionally misconstrued. The conservation and extension of slavery is a matter which lies near the Doctor's heart. He urged secession for the purpose of extending and perpetuating for ever the peculiar institution. His views, however, must have undergone a radical change since the writing of the Cincinnati letter, as he then regarded slavery with little favour. Love of public favour may have much to do with his recently expressed views, for no true Christian and patriot can wish to perpetuate and extend an institution founded on the total subversion of the rights of man.

## REV. DR. JOHN N. WADDELL.

Dr. Waddell is a man of considerable talent, but his prejudices are very strong against the North. He cordially hates a Yankee, and his poor distressed wife, who was a native of New England, was compelled to return to her home, where she mourns in virtual widowhood her unfortunate connection with a man who detests her land and people. Dr. Waddell's sermons are very abusive. The North is the theme of animadversion in all the published sermons and addresses I have seen from his prolific pen. He has prostituted his fine talents, and his writings are full of cursing and bitterness. As President of La Grange College, Tennessee, he might wield a great influence for good—an influence which would tend to calm the storm aroused by demagogues, rather than increase its power. His memory will rot, for the evil which he has done will live after him.

### MAJOR-GENERAL WILLIAM NELSON.

I met General Nelson frequently at his headquarters at Iuka Springs, Mississippi. Though the General was quite brusque in his manners, yet he always treated me with kindness and marked attention. Once while seated at the table with him, several guests being present, the following colloquy ensued.

"Parson Aughey, I suppose you are well versed in the Scriptures, and in order to test your knowledge, permit me to ask a question, which doubtless you are able to answer."

"Certainly, General, you have permission to ask the question you propose. I am not so sure, however, about my ability to answer it."

"The question I desire to propose is this—How many preceded Noah in leaving the ark?"

"I am unable to answer, sir."

"That is strange, as the Bible so plainly and explicitly informs us. We are told that Noah went *forth* out of the ark; therefore *three* must have preceded him."

The General's wit "set the table in a roar." As soon as the mirth had subsided, I addressed the General:

"It is my turn to ask a question. Do you know, sir, where the witch of Endor lived?"

"I did know, but really I have forgotten."

"Well, sir, she lived at Endor."

The laugh was now against him, but he joined in it heartily himself.

Knowing that General Nelson had visited every quarter of the globe, I asked him whether he had ever seen any of the modern Greeks.

"I never saw any of the ancient Greeks," was his curt reply.

General Nelson was regarded as a brave and skilful officer. He has done good service in his country's cause. At Shiloh his promptness and efficiency contributed greatly to retrieve the disaster which befell General Grant on the first day of the battle. His rencontre with General Davis, which resulted in his own death, is greatly to be regretted, though his own ungovernable temper and inexcusable conduct caused his tragic end.

I once visited his headquarters late in the afternoon. On my arrival, he informed me that I would confer a great favour upon him by guiding a company of cavalry on an expedition to the south-eastern part of the county, to which I consented. I rode in front with the officer in command. When we had reached a point beyond the pickets, my companion informed me that we would meet no more Federals; if we met any soldiers while outward bound, we might take it for granted that they were rebels. After riding about an hour longer, we encountered a company of cavalry, and were ordered to halt by the officer in command. My companion, stating that they must be rebels, rode up and gave the countersign. I felt somewhat uneasy at the head of that company at this time, not knowing the moment that bullets would be whistling around us. They proved however to be Federals, returning from an extended scouting expedition. I conducted our company to the house of a Union man, whom we aroused from his bed; and learning that we were Federals, he took my place, and I returned to General Nelson. The General now desired me to go as a spy, to obtain information as to the number of troops stationed at Norman's Bridge, which spanned Big Bear Creek. I replied that I had ridden sixty miles without sleep, but that I would send two Union men of my acquaintance in my stead. This was satisfactory, and my Union friends returned with accurate information as to the number of rebel troops stationed at the bridge, and the best points of attack. The attack was made on the next day after receiving the information, and the rebels were surprised and totally defeated; but few escaped death or capture.

## GENERAL W. T. SHERMAN.

On the day that General Sherman reached Rienzi, I supped with him at the house of a friend. At table the following dialogue took place between us.

"Are you the person from whom Sherman's battery took its name?"

"I am, sir."

"Many gentlemen in this county," said I, "and among them my father-in-law, have pipes made of the fragments of the gun-carriages of Sherman's battery, which was captured at Manassas by the Confederates."

"Sherman's battery was not captured at Manassas," replied the General.

"The honour of capturing Sherman's battery is generally accorded to the second regiment of Mississippi volunteers, which went from this county and the adjoining county of Tippah, though several regiments claim it, and many of my friends declare that they have seen Sherman's battery since its capture."

"I assure you, sir, Sherman's battery was not

captured—so far from this, it came out of the battle of Manassas Plains with two pieces captured from the enemy, having itself lost none."

At this moment Colonel Fry, who killed Zollikoffer, rode up for orders. While receiving them, the horses attached to a battery halted in front of us. "There," said the General, "is every piece of Sherman's battery. I ought to know that battery, and I assure you there is not a gun missing."

The pipes, canes, and trinkets supposed to be made of the wood of Sherman's battery, if collected, would form a vast pile; and were you to inform the owners of those relics that they were spurious, you would be politely informed that you might "tell that tale to the marines," as their sons and their neighbours' sons were the honoured captors of that battery; a fact, concerning the truth of which they entertained not even the shadow of a doubt.

## CHAPTER IX.

### CONDITION OF THE SOUTH.

**Cause of the Rebellion—Prevalence of Union Sentiment in the South—Why not Developed—Stevenson's Views—Why Incorrect—Cavalry Raids upon Union Citizens—How the Rebels employ Slaves—Slaves Whipped and sent out of the Federal Lines—Resisting the Conscript Law—Kansas Jayhawkers—Guarding Rebel Property—Perfidy of Secessionists—Plea for Emancipation—The South Exhausted—Failure of Crops—Southern Merchants Ruined—Bragg Prohibits the Manufacture and Vending of Intoxicating Liquors—Its Salutary Effect.**

THE following is the substance of addresses delivered by me on October 22d and 25th, 1862, at Cooper's Institute, New York, and before the Synod of New York and New Jersey, at its session in Brooklyn.

I will confine myself to rendering answers to various questions which have been asked me since my escape to the North. I have viewed the rebellion from a southern stand-point; have been conversant with its whole history; have been behind the curtains, and have learned the motives which impel its instigators in their treasonable designs against the Government.

Slavery I believe to have been the sole cause of the rebellion. It is true that the slaveholders of the South were becoming strongly anti-republican. Rule or ruin was their determination, and they would not have listened to any compromise measure after the election of Mr. Lincoln; but this feeling, this opposition to republicanism, and lust of power, is the offspring of slavery. In 1856 I heard Jeff. Davis declare that the people of the North and the South were not homogeneous, and that therefore he advocated secession. The reason he assigned for this want of homogeneousness was found in the fact that the South held slaves; the North did not.

Men accustomed to exercise arbitrary power over their fellow-men, will not cease their encroachments upon the rights of all with whom they are associated, politically or otherwise, and a temporary suspension of the control of the government is regarded by them as a *casus belli.* Slavery may therefore be justly regarded as the parent of secession. Whilst this cause exists, the South will be the hot-bed of treason. Slavery has produced its legitimate fruit, and treason is its name. With slavery intact, no compromise, if accepted by the South, would prevent another outbreak in a few years.

The question has been asked, is there any Union sentiment in the South? I reply that there is a strong Union sentiment, even in Mississippi. This sentiment is not found amongst the slaveholders, for, as a class, they are firmly united in their hostility to the Government. The middle and lower classes are not only opposed to secession, but also to slavery itself. Eleven years' association with the southern people has enabled me to form a correct opinion, and to know whereof I affirm. I make this statement without fear of successful contradiction, that the majority of the white inhabitants of the South are Union-loving men. The slaveholders have long ruled both the blacks and the whites in the South. When the rebellion was determined upon, the slaveholders had the organized force to compel acquiescence upon the part of those who favoured the Union, yet wished to remain neutral. Their drafts and conscriptions swept them into the army, and when once there, they must obey their officers upon pain of death. To desert and join the Union army, was to abandon their homes and families, and all their youthful associations. Yet many have done it, and are now doing good service in their country's cause.

The rebels punished with death any who declared himself in favour of the Union. In my presence at Tupelo, they were taken out daily and shot for the expression of sentiments adverse to the rebellion. If the Union troops at any time occupied a place, and the people expressed any favourable sentiments to their cause, upon the evacuation of that position, those who sided with the Union troops were cruelly treated. All these causes, and many others which I might mention, have prevented the full development of the true sentiments of the people. I could name many localities within the rebel lines where the great majority of the people bitterly denounce the Southern Confederacy and all connected with it. I could name many individuals who have declared to me that they would prefer death to a dishonourable compliance with the conscript law. I could name localities within the rebel lines where armed resistance to the conscript law has been made; but the safety of those loyal citizens forbids it.

I know that there are some who assert that there is no Union feeling in the South; but they are mistaken. The author of "Thirteen Months in the Rebel Army" found but little. His situation was not favourable for its discovery. He informs us in his work, that after he had been compelled to *volunteer*, he regarded his oath (an oath much more honoured in the breach than in the observance,) of such force that he sought to obtain information, rather than to desert. He passed from one post of preferment to another, till at length he was on duty under the eye of Breckinridge himself, who complimented him upon his alacrity in bearing dispatches; and this was truly great, as he rode at one time sixty miles in seven hours, and at another, fourteen miles in less than fifty minutes. He also exhibited a guarded zeal for the secession cause. Who would have gone to an officer who was apparently aiding and abetting the rebellion, ably and assiduously, to communicate his Union sentiments? Any who would thus betray themselves could not be sure that they would not be shot in twenty-four hours. Had Mr. Stevenson been with me in Tupelo, and looked upon those seventy or eighty prisoners who were incarcerated for their adherence to the Union—had he witnessed the daily execution of some of them who preferred death to *volunteering* to defend a cause which they did not hesitate to denounce at the peril of their lives—had he been with me while in the midst of a host of Union citizens of Mississippi, who at the noon of night had assembled in the deep glens and on the high hills, for the purpose of devising means to resist the hated conscript law—he would have come to a far different conclusion. I have seen the cavalry go out to arrest Union men. I was at a Mr. William Herron's, in South Carroll, Carrol county, Tennessee, and while there, several companies of cavalry came up from Jackson to destroy the loyal citizens of that vicinity, and they did destroy some of them and much property. They passed within two hundred yards of fortifications hastily thrown up to resist them, and would have been fired on had they come within range. Before completing their mission, a messenger came to inform them that Fort Henry was beleagured. They hastened to the fort just in time to take part in the action. After the surrender of the fort, they retreated to Fort Donelson, and were all captured at the reduction of that fort, to the great joy of those Union citizens whom they had driven from their homes, and whose property they had destroyed.

The slaves add greatly to the strength of the rebellion. Slave labour is extensively employed in the military department. They are the sappers and miners, the cooks, the teamsters, the artisans; and there are instances where they are forced to shoulder the musket and go into the ranks. I have seen and conversed with slave soldiers who have fought in every battle from Manassas to Shiloh.

Many strong secession counties send more soldiers to the rebel army than there are voters in those counties. The slaves who remain at home, labour to raise provisions for the sustenance of the families of the soldiers, and a surplus for the army; hence every white man is available for service in the field. Were this slave labour diverted to some other channel, the result would follow, that a great proportion of the rebel soldiers would be forced to return home to care for their families, or those families must perish. In order to divert this labour, it would be only necessary to encourage the negroes to leave their masters. Wherever the Federal army has advanced in the southwest, the slaves have crowded into their lines by hundreds, and only desisted upon learning, much to their regret, that they would not be received, many of them being tied up and whipped, and then sent southward beyond the limits of the Federal army. Some who had travelled seventy miles upon the underground railroad, to reach the Union army, being asked by their fellow-servants upon their return, how they liked the Yankees, replied that "General Nelson sort o' hinted that he didn't want us." Upon being urged to be more explicit, and to state more fully what was the nature of the hint which led them to infer that General Nelson did not want them, their spokesman replied: "Well, if we must tell, we must. General Nelson tied us up and gave us fifty apiece, and sent us off, sw'arin' he'd guv us a hundred ef we didn't go right straight back home to our masters. He said this wa'n't no war got up to set the niggers free."

The Kansas Jayhawkers liberate all the slaves with whom they come in contact. I passed four regiments of their cavalry last August, on their way to Rienzi, Mississippi. They had about two thousand slaves with them, of every age and sex. Those slaves groomed their horses, drove their wagons, cooked their victuals, and made themselves useful in a variety of ways, leaving every white man free to go into the battle when the hour of contest arrived.

Slavery is a strong prop to the rebellion. Four millions of labourers are able to furnish supplies for eight millions. Subtract that vast resource from the rebellion, add it to the support of the Government, and its stunning effect would be speedily demonstrated in the complete paralysis of the Southern Confederacy. In order to supply the loss of the slaves, half the soldiers in the army must return, or famine would sweep both the army and the families of the soldiers from the face of the earth. One cause of the long continuance of the war is, that the Union army has endeavoured to conciliate the South, rather than crush the rebellion. They have guarded the property of the rebels; they have returned promptly their fugitive slaves; they have put down servile insurrection with an iron hand, and in every possible way have shown clemency instead of severity. But their kindness has been abused, their clemency regarded as evidence of imbecility, and the humane policy of the Government totally misconstrued. Captain John Rainey, of Cambridge, Ohio, while on duty at Corinth, Mississippi, received an application from a notorious secessionist for a guard to protect his premises, which was obtained for him from the colonel, three soldiers being detached for that purpose, who proceeded to the station assigned them. About four o'clock in the afternoon they saw the owner of the premises they were guarding, mount his horse and ride off. Supposing him to be going on some ordinary errand, they took no further notice of it. About nine o'clock, one of the guard who had strayed into the orchard, some three hundred yards from the house, heard an unusual sound, as of cavalry approaching. Concealing himself, he saw, by the bright moonlight, this secessionist ride up with seven or eight rebel cavalrymen, who, seizing his two companions, rode off with them as prisoners. The ingrate who committed this base and perfidious act then went into his house and retired to rest. As speedily as possible the third picket returned to his company, and informed them of the occurrence. Fired with indignation, twenty men volunteered to visit summary punishment upon the perpetrator of this villany. Hastening to his house, they aroused him from his slumbers, and in a few minutes suspended him by the neck between the heavens and the earth. On their return they reported to their companions what they had done, and, through fear of punishment, took every precaution to prevent the act reaching the colonel's ears. It was reported to the colonel, however, whose reply to his informant was, "Served him right!" This policy of guarding rebel property by Union troops must be abandoned, or the war will never terminate. The Union army has been attacked by the rebels when large numbers of the soldiers were absent as guards to protect the plantations and all the interests of secessionists. Such gingerly warfare must end, or the days of the Republic are numbered. Carrying the war into the enemy's country has thus far proved a mere farce. The retreating rebels destroyed tenfold more property than the pursuing Federals. I would not counsel cruelty. I would not advise the unnecessary destruction of life or property, for all wanton destruction tends to weaken rather than to strengthen the cause of those who perpetrate it. Vandalism is everywhere reprehensible. The proper policy I believe to be this: Let the Union army be supplied with provisions, so far as practicable, from the territory occupied. Let the slaves find protection and employment on their arrival within the Union lines. Despise not their valuable services. Let it be proclaimed that for every Union citizen of the South who is slain for his adherence to the old flag, a rebel prisoner shall be executed, and that the confiscated property of Union men shall be restored, at the cost of rebel sympathizers in the vicinity. Let these necessary measures be carried out, and no well-informed person can doubt that the war will cease before the end of six months. With slavery, the rebels are powerful; without it, they are powerless. With slavery, every white man between the ages of eighteen and sixty is available as a soldier, and vast supplies are procured by servile labour. Abolish slavery, and the army would be immediately reduced one-half, and supplies would be diminished to a destructive extent. Slaves armed and drilled would make effective soldiers. With a perfect knowledge of the country, with an intense desire to liberate themselves and their brethren from bondage, with an ardent hatred of their cruel masters and overseers, (and the majority of them are cruel,) they would render a willing and powerful aid in crushing the great rebellion. After the war is ended, give them as much land as their necessities require, either in New Mexico or Arizona, and they will furnish more sugar, rice, and cotton, than were extorted from them by compulsory labour in the house of bondage.

The desire for freedom on the part of the slaves is universal. It is, according to my observation and full belief, a rule without exception. These aspirations are constantly increasing as the rigours of slavery are increased, and the slaves are as well prepared for freedom as they would be a hundred years hence. The *Iron Furnace* of slavery does not tend to the elevation of its victims. There are better methods of elevating a race than by enslaving it. The moral elevation of the slave is no part of the reason why he is held in bondage; but the convenience and profit of the master is the sole end and aim of the peculiar institution. All attempts on the part of the slaves to obtain their liberty are resisted by the slaveholders, by the infliction of appalling and barbarous cruelties. Thirty-two negroes were executed at Natchez, Mississippi, recently, because they expressed a determination "to go to Lincoln." Six were hanged in Hoxubee county, and one burned in the streets of Macon. The southern papers state that Hon. Mr. Orr, of South Carolina, attempted to drive his slaves into the interior, to prevent their escaping to the Yankees, and upon their refusal to go, he ordered them to be driven at the point of the bayonet, and in the execution of the order, fifty of them were slain. There are instances in which the slave is greatly attached to his master's family, but his love of liberty is greater than that attachment. It often transcends his love for his own family, which he abandons for its sake, risking his life on the underground railroad, and enduring the rigours of a Canadian winter, that he may enjoy his inalienable rights.

The southwest is already nearly exhausted. The troops which first went into the service were well supplied with clothing, provisions, and money; but the conscripts were poorly clad, and received their wages in Confederate bonds, which have so depreciated, that ten dollars in gold will purchase one hundred dollars of the bonds. Great suffering is the consequence, and desertions are of daily occurrence. While I was in prison at Tupelo, eighty-seven of the Arkansas infantry deserted in a body. One hundred cavalry were sent to arrest them, but they defeated the cavalry in a fair fight, and went on their way rejoicing. Tennesseeans and Kentuckians could not be trusted on picket duty, their proclivity for desertion being notorious. They suffered no opportunity to escape them, and often went off in squads. Many of them being forced into the service, did not consider their involuntary oath binding.

The wheat crop of 1862, in the southwest, was almost totally destroyed by the rust, and the corn crop by the drought. Salt could not be obtained at any cost, and every marketable commodity had reached a fabulous price. Southern merchants feel that they are ruined. At the commencement of the war they had made large purchases in the North, mainly on credit. The rebel Congress passed a law that all who were indebted to the North must pay two-thirds of the amount of their indebtedness to the Southern Confederacy. This the merchants did. They then sold their goods, taking cotton and Confederate money in pay. The cotton was destroyed by order of Beauregard, and the Confederate scrip is worthless, and the Federal generals are enforcing the payment of Northern claims. This fourfold loss will beggar every southern merchant subjected to it.

At the commencement of the war, strong drink was abundant, and it was freely used by the soldiers. Drunkenness was fearfully prevalent. This vice increased to such a degree that the army was rapidly becoming demoralized. A large amount of grain was wasted in the manufacture of liquor. At this juncture the rebel government wisely prohibited the manufacture and sale of all that would intoxicate. Soon the wisdom of this measure was apparent. For a time this contraband article was smuggled in, yet it was only in limited quantities, and at the present time a drunken soldier is a *rara avis* in the army. At the first promulgation of the law, a cunning countryman perforated a large number of eggs, withdrew the contents, filled the shells with whiskey, closed them up, and carrying them to the camp at Rienzi, sold them at an exorbitant price. Others resorted to filling coffee-pots with whisky, stopping up the bottom of the spout, filling it with buttermilk, and if asked by the guards what they had for sale, would pour out some of the milk in the spout, and by this deception gain an entrance to the camp, and supply the soldiers with liquor. But all these tricks were discovered, and since the manufacture, as well as the sale, was prohibited, the supply on hand became exhausted, and drunkenness ceased.

## CHAPTER X.

### BATTLES OF LEESBURG, BELMONT, AND SHILOH.

**Rebel Cruelty to Prisoners—The Fratricide—Grant Defeated—Saved by Gunboats—Buell's Advance—Railroad Disaster—The South Despondent—General Rosecrans—Secession will become Odious even in the South—Poem.**

### BATTLE OF LEESBURG.

THE battle of Leesburg was fought on the 21st of October, 1861. The southern accounts of this battle were so contradictory, that I will not give the various versions. One statement, however, all concur in—that when the Federal troops retreated to the river, after being overpowered by superior numbers, and had thrown down their arms, calling for quarter, no mercy was shown them. Hundreds were bayoneted, or forced into the river and drowned. The rebels clubbed their guns, and dashed out the brains of many while kneeling at their feet and imploring mercy. I saw one ruffian who boasted that he had bayoneted seven Yankee prisoners captured on that occasion.

### BATTLE OF BELMONT.

The battle of Belmont was fought on the 7th of November, 1861. I have heard repeatedly from southern officers their version of the events which occurred on that occasion. General McClernand, for the purpose of breaking up the rebel camp at Belmont, attacked it in force at an early hour, and completely routed the enemy, pursuing them to a considerable distance. Returning, he destroyed completely the camp, but delaying too long, large reinforcements were thrown over the river from Columbus, and the Federals were compelled to retreat precipitately to their boats, not, however, till they had fully accomplished the object of their mission. A scene occurred on this field which exhibits one of the saddest phases of this internecine strife. The incident was related to me by Mr. Tomlin, a lawyer of Jackson, Tennessee, not unknown even in the North, who was personally acquainted with the actors. Colonel

Rogers, of an Illinois regiment, led his command into action early in the contest. A Tennessee regiment opposed him with fierceness for some time. At length they began to waver and exhibit symptoms of disorder. At this moment their colonel, who had been unhorsed, mounted a stump, and by an energetic and fervid address, rallied his men. Again they began to falter, and again his burning words restored order. Colonel Rogers believing that the safety of himself and regiment depended upon the death of the Tennessee colonel, drew a pistol from his holsters, rode up and deliberately shot him through the brain. The Tennesseeans seeing their colonel fall, fled precipitately. On the return of the Illinois troops, Colonel Rogers, impelled by curiosity, dismounted, and scanning the features of the colonel whom his own hand had slain, recognised his own brother. As the tide of battle had rolled past for the moment, he ordered the corpse to be conveyed to a transport, on which it was brought to Cairo, and thence borne to the stricken parents, who mourned over and buried the remains of their brave but erring child, who had met his fate at his brother's unconsciously fratricidal hand.

## BATTLE OF SHILOH.

On April 6th, 1862, the sun rose clear; not a cloud was discernible in the sky; it was truly a lovely Sabbath, even for a southern clime. Early in the morning I took a walk with my little daughter, a child four years of age, in whose prattle I was taking great interest. We had gone about one hundred yards when my child exclaimed, "Pa, we must go back! it's going to rain; don't you hear the thunder?" The sharp and stunning reports I soon recognised to be the sound of cannon on the field of battle. The cannonading continued incessantly during the day. The whole country became intensely excited, and many citizens hastened to the battlefield, the majority bent upon plunder. On Monday the battle still raged with increasing fury. On Sabbath, General Grant had been completely surprised, and would have lost his whole army but for the gunboats in the river.

These gunboats shelled the pursuing rebels, checking their advance, and saving the discomfitted Federals. Buell arrived with his division on Sabbath night, and on Monday the rebels were driven at every point during the whole day, with great loss. When I heard the rebel officers state that the gunboats lying in the Tennessee river had checked their pursuit, and had committed great havoc amongst their troops, at the distance of nearly three miles, I supposed that the rebel army had continued the pursuit till they came in sight of the gunners on the boats, who then threw their shells into their advancing columns, and my mistake was not corrected till I saw the scene of action. A plateau extended from the river, where the gunboats lay, to the hills, a distance of about one-quarter of a mile. The hills rose to a considerable height, and were covered with a large growth, and on their frowning summits the lofty trees seemed to intercept the passing clouds. Grant's discomfitted and shattered army had taken refuge on the plateau. Some had even thrown themselves into the river, and swam across. Such was the position of affairs when the gunners threw their shells over those lofty hills, and beyond them a distance of two miles, into the midst of the rebels, checking their advance, and destroying them by scores. Couriers constantly passed to and fro to give information of the position of the enemy. All night long their shelling continued, causing Beauregard to change his camp thrice. Thus,

> "Bombs bursting in air,
> Gave proof through the night
> That our flag was still there."

On Monday morning Buell's division advanced, and the tide was turned. The rebels were driven from every position, and their loss was fearful; and had pursuit been continued to Corinth, their whole army must have been annihilated. General A. S. Johnson fell about three o'clock on the Sabbath. The tibial artery had been severed—a wound not necessarily fatal; but he remained in the saddle till he fainted from loss of blood, and when borne from his horse by Governor Harris and others, survived but twenty minutes. On Sabbath night Beauregard occupied, for a time, an old Presbyterian church—a rude log edifice. The church was named Shiloh; hence both Beauregard and General Grant, in their dispatches, named the engagement the battle of Shiloh. I was in Rienzi as the wounded passed down on the cars to the various hospitals below. They passed continually for a month. On the 18th of April I went down to Macon, in Noxubee county. A large number of wounded were on the train. A lady from the Female Seminary in Aberdeen had been placed under my care. When we reached a point six miles from Crawfordsville, I noticed a young man looking out in an excited manner, and immediately after he jumped out and rolled down an embankment. I was much surprised at his conduct, but soon the crashing of the cars explained the cause. The train had been thrown from the track, and was rushing down an embankment. Jumping from the cars now became general. My lady friend arose, declaring that she also would leap from the car. I caught and held her till the danger was over, and thus prevented perhaps serious injury to her person, as all who jumped from the train were more or less injured. On extricating ourselves from the debris of the cars, an appalling sight met our view. The sick, wounded, dying, and dead, were scattered promiscuously in every direction. Their groans and piercing shrieks were heart-rending. The heavy fragments of the broken cars were thrown upon their mangled limbs, and in many instances this disaster completed what Shiloh had commenced. As we came down, I passed through the train amongst the wounded. Some had lost an arm, several an upper lip, as many an under lip. Through the body of one six balls had passed. They were wounded in the feet, the hands, the head, and the body; and some who had not been touched by ball or bullet were paralyzed by their proximity to the exploding shells. Truly every battle is with confused noise and garments rolled in blood. I remained some time at the destroyed train, aiding in extricating those buried beneath the ruins. The extent of the damage and destruction of life, I never accurately learned. It must, however, have been great. The catastrophe was occasioned by a stick of wood falling from the tender before the wheels of the adjacent car, which, being thrown from the track, precipitated the whole train down the embankment.

For weeks after the battle of Shiloh, little was done by Federals or Confederates. The rebels firmly believed that Corinth could not be taken. Its evacuation discouraged the people exceedingly. Nothing but disasters had befallen them since the year commenced. Zollikoffer had been slain, and Crittenden defeated, at Fishing Creek. Roanoke Island had been captured. Forts Henry, Donelson, Pulaski, St. Philip, and Jackson had been reduced. Island "No. 10" was taken, and New Orleans had fallen. The bloody field of Shiloh had proved disastrous; and now, even Corinth, the boasted Gibraltar of rebeldom, fortified by the "best engineer on the continent," and defended by the whole army of the southwest, had been evacuated. What, under these circumstances, could resist the progress of Halleck to the

Gulf? Many saw the cause of these disasters in the fact that the rebel generals had made their attacks upon the Union troops upon the Sabbath; and all history confirms the truth that the army attacking on the Sabbath is almost invariably defeated. Universal gloom and an all-pervading spirit of despondency, brooded over the whole southern people. Had the rebel army been crushed at Corinth, or had Beauregard been vigorously pursued, and forced to fight or surrender, the war in the southwest would have been terminated. General Rosecrans informed me that they could have crushed the rebels at Corinth, and on my asking him why it was not done, he replied: "It would have been done at the cost of many lives on both sides, and it is not our desire to sacrifice life unnecessarily. Let Beauregard go down to the swamps of Mississippi; he can do us no injury. It is not probable that he will ever return to Corinth to attack us, and they must starve out in a section which never produced enough to sustain its own population." But Beauregard did not remain long in the swamps of Mississippi. He took the flower of his army and hastened on to Richmond, to reinforce General Lee, who immediately gave battle to McClellan, and drove him from the Peninsula. Halleck should never have suffered McClellan to be compelled to fight both Lee's forces and Beauregard's, whilst his own army was merely protecting rebel property and consuming rations. I think General Rosecrans, had he been in chief command, would not have thus acted; and his statement to me was a mere apology for the conduct of his superior, for his policy has ever been vigorous, and the rebels dread him more than any living man. The lamented Lyon also inspired a similar wholesome dread. I saw much of General Rosecrans. He is a genial, pleasant gentleman. He seems desirous of accomplishing his end by the use of mild means; but if these will not effect the object, the reverse policy is resorted to. The rebels dread, yet respect him. He will do much to oblige a friend. I desired at one time to go with my family beyond the Federal lines. General Rosecrans went in person to General

Pope to obtain a pass; but Pope's orders were that no passes should be issued for a specified time. General Rosecrans then asked and obtained permission to send one of his aids with us, who conducted us beyond the pickets, a distance of five miles. This act, the General remarked, was in consideration of the kindness I had shown himself and staff while in Rienzi. The Federal generals committed a great mistake in desiring to overrun the country without destroying the rebel armies. A physician who drives a disease from one limb only to appear in a more aggravated form in another, accomplishes nothing. And when a general permits a hostile army to change its location as a strategic movement, he has accomplished nothing, except giving aid and comfort to the enemy. The rebels estimated their forces at the battle of Shiloh at eighty thousand. Though considerable accessions had been received, yet in consequence of sickness and desertion, their number was about the same at the evacuation of Corinth. They lost about eleven thousand, slain, wounded, and prisoners, in the battle.

War has a tendency to engender great bitterness of feeling between the belligerents. The secessionists hate the northern people, but not with the intensity of hatred which they exercise toward the Union-loving citizens of the South. In South Carolina, in the days of nullification, the nullifiers and Union men were very bitter in their hostility against each other. After the suppression of nullification by General Jackson, the cause being removed, the enmity ceased, and in a short time, the odium attached to nullification became so great, that few would admit that they had been nullifiers. Let the supremacy of the law and the Constitution be enforced, and a few years hence, few, even in the South, will be found willing to admit that they were secessionists. The descendants of the Tories carefully conceal their genealogy; the descendants of the secessionists will do the the same. Slavery and secession will perish together; and the classes of the South who have been fearfully injured by both these heresies, will be fully compensated for their present distress by the vast blessings which will accrue to themselves and posterity by the abolition of an institution which has degraded labour, oppressed the poor white man, opposed progress, retarded the development of the country's resources, taken away the key of knowledge, caused every species of vice to flourish, impoverished the people, enriched a favoured class at the expense of the masses, caused woes unnumbered to a whole race—in short, has been the prolific parent of fraud, oppression, lust, tyranny, murder, and every other crime in the dark catalogue.

"We are living, we are dwelling
In a grand and awful time;
In an age, on ages telling,
To be living is sublime!

Hark! the waking up of nations,
Gog and Magog to the fray;
Hark! what soundeth—is creation
Groaning for its latter day?

Will ye play, then? will ye dally
With your music and your wine?
Up! it is Jehovah's rally!
God's own arm hath need of thine.

Hark! the onset! will ye fold your
  Faith-clad arms in lazy lock;
Up! oh, up! thou drowsy soldier,
  Worlds are charging to the shock!

Worlds are charging; heaven beholding;
  Thou hast but an hour to fight;
Now the blazoned cross unfolding,
  *On!* right onward *for the right.*

*On!* let all the soul within you,
  For the truth's sake go abroad;
Strike! let every nerve and sinew
  Tell on ages,—tell for God!"

CPSIA information can be obtained
at www.ICGtesting.com
Printed in the USA
LVHW100442110522
718424LV00003B/203

9 783375 002190